She had used it only a handful of times. But Kira was directly challenging her authority, and she wouldn't wait a nanosecond to stop her.

The sceen remained gray for several heartbeats, until Worf's head appeared. There was a long scratch near his mouth, and when he spoke she could see blood on his teeth, indicating he had been hit hard enough to break flesh.

"Who disturbs me!" he roared into the screen. B'Elanna recognized the blood lust in his eyes. Over his shoulder, she could see a vague form with curling dark hair falling down her back. At least he wasn't with Kira.

"My apologies," B'Elanna said quickly. "But Kira has stolen two Vulcan eunuchs from the shrine—"

"You bother me about *'Iw-slaves!'*" Worf was already looking back at Troi, distracted from B'Elanna. She knew she only risked infuriating him by pressing it now.

"I have to return to Mars immediately," B'Elanna told him instead. "I need to work on the Earth deep-core mining—"

"Then do it," Worf interrupted.

"Shall I inform Koloth to accompany the *Sitio?*" B'Elanna asked, holding firm.

"Yes. Worf out."

The screen went black, and B'Elanna slammed both her fists into the top of the desk. Even when she was right, she was stifled at every turn!

But she swore, in the end, she would make Kira pay.

STAR TREK®

BOOK

DARK PASSIONS

two

SUSAN WRIGHT

POCKET BOOKS

New York   London   Toronto   Sydney   Singapore

An *Original* Publication of POCKET BOOKS

POCKET BOOKS, a division of Simon & Schuster, Inc.
1230 Avenue of the Americas, New York, NY 10020

Copyright © 2001 by Paramount Pictures. All Rights Reserved.

STAR TREK is a Registered Trademark of Paramount Pictures.

A VIACOM COMPANY

This book is published by Pocket Books, a division of Simon & Schuster, Inc., under exclusive license from Paramount Pictures.

ISBN: 0-671-78786-1

First Pocket Books printing January 2001

10 9 8 7 6 5 4 3 2 1

Printed in the U.S.A.

Acknowledgment

Thanks to John Ordover for his brilliant idea to feature the powerful women of *Star Trek* in a novel set in the Mirror Universe.

The setting for *Star Trek: Dark Passions* Books One and Two is the dark, intense "Mirror Universe" as established on *Star Trek: Deep Space Nine,* and reflects the lifestyles and mores of that universe. The players are not the Star Trek characters as we have come to know them, but their harder, crueler, alternate universe equivalents.

The date is sometime before Major Kira and Dr. Bashir rediscovered this harsh realm where humans are enslaved by a Klingon, Cardassian, and Bajoran alliance; where no one knows whom to trust.

Chapter 1

FOR THE FIRST time, Deanna Troi was uncomfortable on the bridge of the *Negh'Var,* the flagship of the Alliance Armada. Next to her, Regent Worf reclined on his imposing command chair. The rest of the Klingon crew stood at their stations around the long narrow bridge.

Troi didn't have a station. As Intendant of Betazed, she wasn't officially part of the *Negh'Var's* crew. Instead, she preferred to stand near the support beams directly to Worf's left, close enough that he could speak to her privately or she could make suggestions. The bridge was darkened except for the display panels, so she was shadowed and thus could observe the officers.

But her joy at being by her *Imzadi* was ruined by the presence of Kira Nerys. Troi had never imagined Kira would join them on the *Negh'Var.*

When Worf had heard that the new Overseer was

making a grand tour of the shipping lines through the former Terran Empire, he changed course to intercept Kira's starship. He insisted he must observe her activities. Troi couldn't argue with that.

Yet within days of meeting up with the *Siren's Song*, Kira's ship was docked in the largest launching bay on board the *Negh'Var*. At eight decks high, the *Siren's Song* was really too big for the cavernous bay, but somehow Kira had wedged it in there. One morning Troi woke up and found that Kira had moved her crew, staff, and slaves into quarters on the *Negh'Var*. She did not appear to be in any hurry to leave.

Kira had even appropriated a spot on the bridge directly opposite from Troi, on the other side of Worf. Whenever Troi looked at Worf, she couldn't help but see Kira, her short red hair incongruous on the somber bridge. It was galling to be outflanked on her own ship. Kira had been nothing but a nuisance since she had become Overseer.

Troi's last attempt at getting rid of Kira had been destroyed by the death of Winn Adami. She wasn't sure who had killed Winn. The only evidence was a Klingon knife. But Troi suspected that Kira had something to do with it. Kira didn't try to hide her satisfaction that her political rival on Bajor was gone.

Suddenly Kira laughed out loud, making a comment about the Dohlman of Elas to Worf. "She acts like a painted replica!"

Troi sensed sexual overtones in Kira's use of the word "replica." It made Troi narrow her eyes while Worf grunted in amusement. A moment ago he had been irritated because the young Dohlman of Elas was resisting his demands for additional vessels to accompany the Armada as an "honor guard" through their sector. But Kira seemed capable of charming Worf at almost any time.

Troi normally would have been enjoying Worf's display of strength in appropriating the Dohlman's vessels. But instead, she hardly paid attention as double disruptor beams suddenly pierced one of the tiny vessels, blowing it up in a burst of blue-orange heat. Sparkling debris showered over the bridge dome, reminding Troi of the gorgeous meteor showers on Betazed II. She had watched them every night from the cliffs of New Hope while she had waited for Worf to return from Bajor last time.

Maybe she was thinking more about the revised plans for New Hope that her architect had sent for approval, because Worf's heart wasn't in this confrontation. Much of his anger had been drained by the glorious battle against the Romulans in the name of Duras. With fresh legions fighting on the front, continuing to press the Romulans back, the victory had been enough to assure Duras a place in Sto'Vo'Kor. Worf had then gone to Terok Nor, where Kira had welcomed the victorious warriors. After he returned, he had actually been . . . mellow.

Troi yawned as the screen showed the proud Elasian beauty humbling herself and begging Worf's forgiveness for the delay. Worf could lay waste to much of the Elasian territory if he chose, but Troi sensed his boredom. He was probably thinking, *Why bother?*

Kira said, "I suppose this means we'll shift the trade

route closer to the Lissepians and choke the Elasians into proper obedience."

Worf agreed, "The Dohlman will learn her place in the Alliance." Without glancing at Troi, he ordered, "Change course to the Lissepian sector."

As Worf's crew instantly obeyed their commander, Troi exerted every bit of empathy she possessed to sense what Kira was feeling now. The Bajoran was excited by Worf's display of power and the destruction of the Elasian vessel. Her fiercely sensual reaction disturbed Troi. It was too much like her own emotional rapport with Worf.

Kira was clearly engaged in a rivalry with her for Worf's attention. In many ways she had already managed to interfere in their relationship. Just last night, shortly after Troi had dismissed Keiko, she and Worf had been interrupted by a request from Kira. Worf had disappeared for almost an hour before returning to her bed.

"Sir!" First Officer Koloth announced. "We are receiving a message from the *Groumall*, requesting permission to rendezvous with the Alliance Armada."

"Gul Dukat!" Kira exclaimed, her voice filled with loathing.

The first officer confirmed, "I have the *Groumall* on long-range sensors."

"Tell him to get lost," Kira said with a wave of her hand. "Who wants him around?"

Worf frowned, pulling thoughtfully on his beard.

Troi felt a quickening of hope. Worf had fallen into the habit of doing whatever Kira suggested. But this time, he clearly thought it wiser to not offend a fellow

Alliance member. From the way he glanced at Kira, he also didn't like her arrogant assumption that he would do whatever she said.

"Request granted," Worf told his first officer.

"But what about the festival you've been planning?" Kira asked sweetly. "Dukat will ruin it."

Worf clearly had not considered the Kot'Baval Festival, but he almost never rescinded an order. He slumped deeper in his chair, scowling. But Kira laughed and shrugged it off. "Who knows? Maybe Dukat will get drunk and turn out to be the life of the party."

Troi could tell that Kira really didn't care about Dukat joining them. Her objection had been as fleeting as her other desires. Troi found that flightiness difficult to understand. As an empath, she was accustomed to judging actions according to people's emotional motivation. But Kira used her feelings as a playground. Emotions were called up and romped around, but nothing was taken seriously. Troi didn't know what was important to Kira, but she was certainly determined to find out. If she didn't do something fast, Kira could fascinate Worf beyond Troi's powers to combat.

The Kot'Baval Festival celebrated the ancient victory of Molar the Unforgettable over Kahless. Worf and one of his strongest warriors reenacted the fifteen-hundred-year-old ritual of Kahless attacking Molar with a strange new weapon called the *bat'leth*. Molar, with his superior strength, wrested the weapon from Kahless and slew the contender for his claim to the Klingon Empire.

Troi's mood was lifted by the high spirits of the Klingon crew, but having seen this particular ritual enacted many times before, she was not really moved. Even with the blade singing through the air, passing within a hairsbreadth of Worf's chest, she was hardly concerned. She knew exactly which move Worf would make to parry the thrust and wrest the *bat'leth* away. She liked things raw and unpredictable, but Worf cherished his rituals.

Now that the battle had been completed, Worf was at the front of the hall, drinking and talking loudly among his warriors. Both men and women butted their heads in merry disregard for their skulls. The smell of sweat and leather competed with the swirling smoke from the lanterns. For a moment, Troi forgot they were on a starship.

The few non-Klingon guests seemed out of place, clearly lacking Troi's unique ability to meld into any situation. Kira Nerys was drinking with the second officer, while her Terran slave solemnly surveyed the riotous crew. A few male Rutians, with their distinctive white streaks of hair, gathered to one side of the hall. They drank large flagons of bloodwine, and seemed to be handling the intoxicant well.

The most unusual presence in the great hall of the flagship was Gul Dukat and his aides. Troi vividly remembered Dukat's reaction at the Alliance gathering when Kira was named Overseer of the fallen Terran Empire. His outrage and sense of betrayal had been palpable, though he hardly moved a muscle. Troi had been pleasantly surprised by his reaction. It was not often that

Cardassians revealed themselves so clearly. Their deceptive natures led them to hide their most cherished desires even from themselves. It was the ultimate way to keep their enemies from discovering their weak points.

So Troi was pleased that Gul Dukat had joined them for the Kot'Baval Festival. Dukat certainly acted like an ally rather than an enemy. His pleasant smile and gently clasped fingers betrayed nothing but polite interest in the ritual. His face was a pale greenish-gray spot among the dark Klingons, and the crew instinctively avoided the table where the Cardassians were seated.

Kira came toward Troi laughing, the effects of the bloodwine clear in her step. But even tipsy, she managed to look seductive with her knowing smile and swaying hips. Kira wore a black skin-suit, similar to the Klingon uniform Troi preferred. So Troi had begun wearing dresses to avoid comparisons. Worf had complimented her on her vibrant blue dress, cut to a deep V over one breast. He had encircled her waist with his hands, lifting her for a kiss. As he swung her around, her hair had loosened and came tumbling down around her shoulders. He insisted she leave the long dark curls free, gently kissing one tress before leaving the privacy of their quarters.

Feeling smug, Troi allowed Kira to approach. The Bajoran had been drinking quite a bit and would perhaps reveal more than she intended.

"Come on, Seven!" Kira called teasingly. Turning to Troi, she added, "She's afraid of you. Afraid you'll read her mind."

"Sorry to disappoint you," Troi told both Kira and the statuesque blond Terran. "But I'm not telepathic."

"Maybe not," Kira agreed. "But everyone says you know what people think." She grabbed Seven's hand and pulled her even closer to Troi. "I bet you can't figure out Seven . . ."

Troi was offended. "She's your Terran slave."

"No!" Kira laughed out loud, drawing attention to them. "Seven's a Free-Terran."

Troi considered Seven in spite of herself. Her own concealed half-Terran heritage usually made her avoid the few Free-Terrans she encountered. At a glance, she could tell this woman was unique. She was quite tall, and dressed for the occasion in a Cardassian military uniform. The strong diagonal lines made a dramatic counterpoint to her serene expression. Her attitude was good—her hands were clasped behind her back and her boots spread as if she was poised to defend herself. Troi could sense a touch of inner uneasiness, though her full lips never trembled. When they began to receive more attention from the boisterous Klingons, Troi got the impression that Seven was always this self-possessed. Several of the Klingons were suggesting, not so quietly, what they could do with a woman like Seven. But the Terran ignored them.

"She's not what she seems," Troi said briefly.

"That's amazing!" Kira exclaimed. "You're right. Seven may look Terran, but she was raised as a Cardassian. I was talking to Gul Dukat over there." She jerked a thumb in his direction. In response, he stood up and began to approach. "He knows the family Seven used to live with. Ghemor is on the Detapa Council now."

"What are you doing so far from Cardassia?" Troi politely asked Seven.

"Nerys invited me to come with her on the tour," Seven replied.

Kira let out an unapologetic yawn as she languorously stretched. "And now it's time to leave. Come on, my dear. The company around here is not to my taste." This last was said with a glance over her shoulder at the approaching Gul Dukat.

Kira glided away before Dukat reached them, swinging her hips in suggestive appeal. Seven supported her arm, staunchly clearing a way through the staggering Klingons. Troi felt no animosity from Kira. There was nothing but curiosity and, after Troi's assessment of Seven, admiration for her empathic skill.

Gul Dukat arrived in time to look after Kira's retreating form. His eye ridges were drawn in displeasure. Troi was reminded of that unguarded moment at the Alliance gathering when his emotions ran strong.

"You are distressed," Troi quietly said.

"No." Dukat quickly covered his momentary lapse of attention with a cordial smile.

"It's natural for you to feel betrayed," Troi assured him. "First Kira seized the Intendant's post without your approval, and now she has taken the Overseer's position from you."

"I was her commanding officer," Dukat said by way of explanation. His urbane demeanor belied his warrior's armor, and she wondered if he was a good fighter. Assessing him quickly, she decided that though he was imposing and physically well-formed, his temperament was compelled toward covert manipulation rather than hand-to-hand combat.

Troi ventured a light laugh. "Perhaps you and Kira were closer than fellow officers."

Now his smile grew cold. "Not likely."

Troi was tempted to push this line of questioning, feeling his response despite his negative reply. He did feel an attraction for Kira, perhaps even tenderness. Unusual for a xenophobic Cardassian.

But before Troi could continue, Dukat gestured. "Look at her with the Regent."

Troi slowly turned, having steeled herself to never reveal her jealousy. That would be her undoing. Yet she knew that she was going to be sorely tested.

Kira was leaning on Worf's arm, her curvaceous body bumping into him as she laughed. Worf supported her when she nearly collapsed in mirth, while he tossed back his head and joined in. Troi so rarely saw Worf laugh, and it made her nervous. He was off his guard tonight, and she knew Kira had something to do with it. The Bajoran certainly was vital, with her unruly red curls barely contained by a new silver foil headband. And she held on to Worf so tightly—

"She flatters men," Dukat was saying bitterly. "She makes them want her, love her, do anything for her. Ironic considering she has always longed for a partner who was stronger than herself."

"Oh?" Troi said, startled from her observation. Could it be true? Was that what Kira wanted?

"Perhaps that blond Terran will finally satisfy her." Dukat almost choked with resentment.

Troi gave Seven another look. She was waiting near Kira, an island of reserve in the midst of the boisterous company. The Cardassian uniform seemed incongruous on a Terran.

"Perhaps." Troi didn't believe that such an aloof young woman could control Kira Nerys. "I don't understand why you're concerned after the way she betrayed you."

"Becoming Overseer is one thing." Dukat was still watching Kira as she slowly detached herself from Worf. She managed to touch him even more as she said good night. "Holding the post is another."

Troi finally began to smile, turning her full attention to Dukat as Kira left Worf alone. "Perhaps we have more in common than I realized."

An eagerness quickened his eye. "There are many who are not pleased with the current situation."

Troi gestured for him to follow her. "Come, let's go where we can talk. . . ."

Chapter 2

KIRA NERYS NEVER lost sight of the fact that Deanna Troi had conspired with Winn Adami to have her killed. Troi had promised to make Winn the Intendant of Bajor after Kira was dead. Kira's primary reason for this "extended tour of her responsibilities" was to neutralize the threat posed by Deanna Troi. Kira believed the Betazoid's power rested on her relationship with Worf. But supplanting Troi was turning out to be more difficult than Kira had assumed it would be.

Kira didn't want to alert the empath that she knew about the assassination attempt, so she did her best to forget about it. Troi wouldn't dare make a move against her while she was on board the *Negh'Var*. So Kira channeled her preoccupation with Troi into curiosity, not bothering to hide her admiration for the elegant woman.

Yet she was continually alert for a weakness in Troi that she could exploit.

Anyway, how could she resent Troi's interference in her life when it had given her Seven? Kira found it highly gratifying to know that she had thwarted an assassination attempt simply through her personal charms. Seven was obviously devoted. It was intoxicating.

All in all, Kira was having a delightful time as Overseer. She loved the way the leaders and officials of every system jumped when she crooked her finger. A few of the Intendants had been sulky or downright hostile, but most understood their place and were overzealous in trying to please her. Kira made sure everyone knew what she wanted, and severely punished those who didn't satisfy her. They gave her presents and bribes until she was afraid the *Siren's Song* wouldn't be able to carry everything back to Bajor. Her quarters on board the *Negh'Var* were hung with precious fabrics and art, and decorated with objects made of rare gems, metals, and crystals. Spices were burned to fill the chambers with soothing scents, each gram worth its weight in latinum.

Her quarters were so sublime that at first she didn't want to leave them. She knew the Regent probably had surveillance on her, and likely Troi had her own system of watching her movements. Kira wasn't used to being watched, and she found it exciting in a subversive kind of way.

But Kira was beginning to wonder when Troi would react. Worf clearly enjoyed her company. Kira took every opportunity to try to lighten his mood after she realized that Deanna Troi had no sense of humor. Apparently it was working, because the Klingon crew was growing more respectful toward her by the day. That was as unlikely, in her opinion, as a Cardassian being honest.

She had even delighted in teasing Gul Dukat at the Kot'Baval Festival by parading Seven around in a Cardassian Gul's uniform. Surely that would get back to Ghemor and the Detapa Council.

Seven was proving to be quite an asset. When Kira's staff had become hopelessly mired in the details of the Overseer's duties, Seven had stepped in and sorted things out. She was quite bright, really, and Kira had gratefully handed over most of the day-to-day duties.

That meant Kira was able to concentrate on the problem of Troi. Every morning, she downloaded the *Negh'-Var*'s general orders to see what was new. Troi routinely involved herself in running the *Negh'Var*, including giving orders to the first officer. Troi was also far more deeply entrenched in Worf's duties as Regent than Kira had anticipated. That would make it more difficult to remove her from his life. But Kira was confident she would win Worf over if she persevered.

So one day, after some midmorning refreshment, the slaves were dressing Kira as she flicked through the daily orders on her padd. A request caught her eye concerning shore leave on Risa. Who wouldn't be curious about the infamous pleasure resort of the fallen Terran Empire? It had been preserved by the Alliance and was kept stocked with the best luxury services and items.

Risa was known throughout the quadrant as the premier planet for shore leave.

Now that she thought about it, Kira wouldn't mind visiting Risa. There was no real need for the Overseer to go there. It was run by the Alliance for the pleasure of Alliance vessels, and was already as tightly regulated as any planet could be. Yet she had a sudden burning desire to see what everyone was talking about.

The request by First Officer Koloth for shore leave on Risa had been denied by Troi. Her grounds were that they would lose six days because of the detour to reach the pleasure planet. The order was acknowledged by the first officer's stamp, but there was no indication that Worf had seen it or approved Troi's "request denied."

Kira hummed to herself as she devised her plan, letting Seven brush her hair and settle the silver foil headband over her forehead. It was one of the presents she had received from the Valtese Intendant. The shimmering material was reportedly worth a small moon. It gave her a distinguished look, and lent her the air of wearing a crown. She liked that, and had decided to adopt it as part of her official Overseer's uniform, along with the black skin-suit and chest harness.

"All of you stay here," Kira ordered the slaves.

"May I come with you?" Seven immediately asked.

"No, you know better than to ask me that!" Kira rarely took her slaves anywhere on the *Negh'Var* because Klingons were known to strike a Terran for simply being there. Kira didn't like anyone to touch her slaves except for her. But Seven wouldn't stop asking to leave their rooms. Now Kira would have to take away one of her privileges for being so presumptuous. But she could deal with Seven later, when she could thoroughly enjoy herself. Right now, she had important matters to take care of.

It was early yet for Troi to be on the bridge. She preferred to arrive after the shift change, when the senior officers were on deck. But Kira had noticed that Worf often went to the bridge in the morning, though he did little more than stare at the stars on the screen. Kira got the impression that the brooding Klingon was never so happy as when he was reclining in the huge command chair, his legs stretched out and his chin planted on his fist, watching the galaxy pass before his eyes.

Kira joined him, stepping up on the platform that raised Worf above everyone else on the bridge. "I could stay out here forever," Kira sighed, leaning against the arm of his chair.

Worf looked at her intently. "What about Bajor?"

"I love being on a starship. It's much more interesting than living on a station that orbits one planet. I've been cooped up for far too long. . . ." Kira gazed at the screen, noting the way he turned toward her. A direct hit. "You love it out here, too."

"Yes." His deep voice carried a finality, emphasizing how much it meant to him.

Kira smiled and let it pass, knowing he would think more of her for it. After a few moments, with a laughing tone, she said, "I know something else you like."

"What?" he asked.

She pursed her lips, suppressing her laughter. "Kling-on opera."

Worf relaxed slightly, as if he had been wary about what she would say. That was good. He was aware of his own attraction to her. "Yes, I appreciate Klingon opera."

"I have an idea that would be fun," Kira said playfully. "Risa is famous for its opera house. We're only a couple of days away, so why not stop in? We could catch the performance of Tow'ga in *Sompek's Revenge*."

"The battle of Tong Vey," Worf murmured, his interest caught.

"I hear the Risa Opera House is bigger than most starships," Kira told him. "They use a thousand extras during the battle, and dozens are killed during the melee every night." She paused, making sure she had his attention. "You would surely get the best seat in the house."

Worf started shaking his head. "I was told the detour would take too long."

"Too long?" Kira said innocently. So Troi did consult with him on the orders. That meant she did not have absolute power on the *Negh'Var.* "Do you have to be somewhere?"

"No," Worf admitted.

"Well, good. Neither do I." When he didn't respond, she added, "I thought the Regent set our course."

Worf sounded defensive. "That is so."

"Then let's go to Risa. It won't even take that long. Let me show you," she offered, pointing to the small screen in the arm of his chair. "Pull up the star chart with our route."

Worf obliged, making Kira smile. Despite his overbearing, dominating behavior, Troi had trained him to take orders very nicely.

"See," Kira said, leaning against his arm as she ran her finger suggestively down the screen. "Our current flight path takes us through the Hekaras Corridor. We'd have to slow to at least warp two to get past the tetryon fields safely. But if we detour toward Risa at warp nine, then we only lose the two days we're on shore leave." She had considerably fudged the numbers, but figured she could pass it off later as confusion with warp conversion rates. "If the Regent can't take two days off, who can?"

Her face was very close to his, but he didn't pull back. He seemed fascinated by her, as if he was too preoccupied with her to listen to what she said. Exactly as she had planned.

"Let's do it," she urged. "Let's go to Risa."

Worf hesitated, but he was unable to deny her. "Yes."

"What fun!" Kira placed her hand on his arm and gave it a squeeze. She let go before Worf could grow uneasy and pull away.

She retreated to her usual post against the support beam where she could see everything. There was nothing else she could do. It was up to Worf whether he would honor his word and change course. She could understand his reluctance. It would countermand a direct order from Deanna Troi. His first officer had already acknowledged that the request was denied.

His silent struggle was highly entertaining. But the lure of Sompek and his own pleasure weighed too heavily on the scale.

Worf summoned his first officer to the command chair. "Change course to Risa and proceed at warp nine. Shore leave will be granted to the crew for two days."

"By your honor, sir!" Koloth replied. But his wide grin said much more. Koloth lost no time in returning to his post and issuing orders to the crew. The Klingons shifted at their posts, looking at one another, obviously enthused about getting shore leave. A charge ran through the bridge that was perceptible. When the shift change occurred, the officers were loudly talking about Risa as they exchanged posts.

Kira wanted to laugh. It was working out so well. Eagerly, she waited for Troi to arrive, concentrating on her anticipation of seeing the hot spot in the Alpha Quadrant. But it also wouldn't hurt to feel a little victorious so Troi would know who was responsible.

When the Betazoid came onto the bridge, everyone was aware of it. She was a delicate woman, yet she had a way of filling a room with her presence. Today she wore a pale shell-pink dress that clung nearly transparent to her ivory skin. Her dark curls were piled high on her head with a few long ringlets dangling carelessly against her neck. She looked like an expensive toy, but Kira knew better than to underestimate her.

Troi sweetly responded to Worf's greeting. He practically stood up when she appeared, then seemed to remember himself, sitting back down. She joined him on the platform, slightly away from the command chair, standing gracefully in her high-heeled boots. Worf didn't move again, his clenched fist resting under his chin as he stared forward. Kira was practically on her toes, eager to see what would happen.

Two of the officers passed by, returning from the replicator at the rear of the bridge with *pipius* tea for Worf and themselves. Kira had refused—she couldn't drink anything made from a creature with claws that big. But the brew appeared to powerfully stimulate Klingons.

One of the crew was quietly chuckling to the other about the pleasure pits on Risa. Worf accepted the flagon of stimulant, ordering them, "Be silent!" As he drank, he glanced over at Troi.

Kira was not pleased by Worf's anxiety. She had been hoping to get a reaction from Troi, not Worf. Clearly he was concerned about what she would think.

Troi gently smiled. "We've changed course for Risa?"

Worf guardedly said, "Yes." He hesitated, but couldn't seem to bear the silence. "We only lose two days by avoiding the Hekaras Corridor."

Kira stepped out of the shadows. "Isn't it exciting? Risa has such fabulous Klingon opera . . ."

Troi betrayed no sign of dismay. She must have known it was Kira's suggestion. And she must feel some chagrin at having her order publicly countermanded. Yet her faint smile indicated she didn't care.

Then Troi leaned over and gently tugged on Worf's whiskers. "You'll enjoy that."

Worf let out a guffaw and planted a kiss on her lips. The rest of the bridge crew were covertly watching, exchanging knowing grins and sneers. The mood on the bridge was infectious, but Kira felt oddly flattened, as if she had missed something important. The way Troi was looking into Worf's eyes made it seem as if Kira had lost, when really she had won. Or had she?

Kira shrugged and left the bridge, returning to her quarters and her warm, agreeable slaves. What did she care about Worf anyway? There had to be another way to get rid of Troi.

She could always use the Iconian portal with its astonishing teleportation power. If she felt her life was in danger, then one dark night she could send someone to pay a visit to Deanna Troi.

Meanwhile, Kira intended to immerse herself in all the pleasures the galaxy offered, including a glorious stay on Risa.

Chapter 3

SEVEN WAS SPENDING most of the long, tedious tour analyzing the volumes of data submitted by the Intendants and planetary officials. Without her cranial implant database, Seven would have been as lost as Kira's staff. But using the Obsidian Order's field analysis program to detect patterns within chaos, Seven was becoming adept at seeing the bottlenecks in trade and production. She was also gathering extremely valuable data for the Obsidian Order. Once her implant was downloaded, Tain would have priceless information about every system in the Alliance territory.

It was a fulfilling way to spend the hours that Kira spent elsewhere. When Kira met with Intendants or planetary officials, she usually chose to have Marani accompany her. Marani had been trained in protocol.

So Seven didn't see Kira very often, but whenever she

did, she tried to please her. Enabran Tain had ordered her to ingratiate herself with the Overseer and report back everything she saw. Seven dutifully complied. She also contained her eagerness to report to Tain about the existence of the ancient teleportation device which had enabled her to pass through the security systems at the Bajoran Ministry complex. The key to successful infiltration was to cut off contact with home base. Soon enough, she would have the opportunity to inform Tain.

Everything would have been satisfactory, except that Seven kept waking up in the night in a soaking sweat. Panic clutched her every time. She kept seeing Winn Adami and heard her say, "You don't want to kill me. I can tell. I used to be like you. . . ."

It unnerved Seven because she had never experienced anything like it before. However, she assumed that retraining would focus her concentration again. Meanwhile, she tried to ignore it.

The dull routine continued until shortly before they arrived at Risa. Benjamin Sisko, the dark Free-Terran who worked for Kira, rendezvoused with the *Negh'Var* as they entered the system. Kira stayed in her quarters for the rest of the day as they approached Risa at impulse power. Sometimes she was alone with Sisko, sometimes not. Under her direction, the slaves packed up many of the precious objects in their cunningly contrived cases, stowing them in enormous titanium cargo cylinders which Kira closed with her own combination and seal.

"These are the last two," Kira told Sisko.

"I'll call my crew," he replied, reclining on the sofa.

Seven was using an antigrav unit to maneuver one of the containers into the center of the room. It was taller than herself and bigger around than her arms could reach.

"You better take them yourself," Kira said flatly. "Seven will help you."

"What?" Sisko demanded lazily. "You want me to lug those things all the way down to the docking bay?"

Kira smiled, leaning over to pat his cheek. "Fine, we'll be entering orbit of Risa shortly. I've been curious whether the Alliance interdiction revoking Free-Terran status on Risa extends to Terrans who are in orbit."

Sisko got up. "It's been charming, as always, Nerys." He stretched, summoning a genuine smile. "But I'll have to be going now."

Kira lifted one side of her mouth, as if amused in spite of herself. "No side trips on the way back, Benjamin. I'm notifying Garak that if you're not there in two weeks, he's to send out search ships to take you into custody."

Sisko raised his brows, but didn't comment on that. "Seven, why are you standing there? Get moving."

Seven drew in her breath, but didn't respond. After spending time with Sisko, she had discovered it was impossible to pierce his indifferent armor. It was better to ignore him. She activated the antigrav unit and leaned into the cylinder to move it out the door.

Despite the presence of Sisko, Seven was eager for this unexpected chance to see more of the flagship of the Alliance. The *Negh'Var* was enormous, the largest starship currently under command in the Alpha Quadrant. On their way down to the docking bays, she noted everything from the width of the corridors and junctions, to the placement of Jefferies tubes and key operational sites such as computer banks and transporter rooms. She compared everything to the information stored in her implant, updating the files on a continuous basis. Other Obsidian Order agents could benefit from this knowledge in the future.

The crew of the *Negh'Var* was entirely Klingon. As the two Terrans proceeded through the corridors, they received many glares and outright displays of bared, dripping teeth. Seven scrupulously avoided looking them in the eye, knowing eye contact would be taken for a challenge. Since they arrived at the docking bay with no incident, she assumed Sisko had taken the same precaution. Indeed, he was unusually subdued by the time they reached the *Denorios*.

Sisko's crew spilled out of the small starship into the active docking bay. Seven was occupied with observing every minute detail of the bay and the ships docked next to one another. Yet she noted that Jadzia was among the crew.

The Trill pilot avoided her, as well she should after raising Kira's suspicions about Seven. Seven looked through Jadzia as if she didn't exist. Trust, once broken, was never regained. Enabran Tain had taught her that, and she had survived by it. Tain had given her life when everyone else had abandoned her, including her Cardassian foster family.

Yet her training was barely enough to hold back her seething anger. It was because of Jadzia's loose tongue that Seven had been forced to reveal her true past. When

Kira had found her Cardassian cranial implant, Seven had to resort to her most basic cover, which contained many elements of truth. She had explained how her Terran parents crash-landed on a Cardassian colony and she had been taken in by Ghemor's family. She even gave Kira her Cardassian citizen's ID number as proof. Tain must know what had happened by now. According to official records, instead of attending the Obsidian Order training facility, Seven had gone to a provincial boarding school, then set herself up as a merchant pilot with monetary help from her Cardassian foster family.

Seven felt as if she was no longer undercover. She was using her own history and her own face as a disguise. It was a violation of everything she had become . . . and suddenly she wasn't sure who she was anymore. She had lived inside a protective shell of otherness for so long that she didn't know how to simply be herself.

Seven tried to calm herself as Sisko ordered his jabbering crew back into the *Denorios* to prepare for immediate departure. They scattered, more than willing to get off the *Negh'Var*, where they had to stay confined to their patrol ship. That left Sisko and Seven to slide the cargo containers through the open hatchway.

Down the short corridor, Seven paused while Sisko went through an elaborate procedure to open the locked cargo bay. He easily pushed his container over the threshold, and was turning for Seven's. She ignored his offer of assistance, still feeling a very un-agent-like resentment toward him.

Inside the cargo bay were eighteen close-packed

cargo containers. They held several fortunes in bribes and gifts. Seven couldn't help glancing speculatively at Sisko. "Some people would consider this very tempting."

Sisko was releasing the antigrav unit on his container, snugging it against two others. "What? You think I'll run off with Kira's knickknacks?"

Seven shrugged, getting a new grip on her container to push it into place. "Kira apparently trusts you."

Sisko stood out of the way. "Why shouldn't she? I'm not going anywhere. Where could I find a better berth than Terok Nor?"

Seven settled her container against the others. She didn't care whether Sisko returned to Terok Nor with Kira's treasures or not.

"Maybe you're the one who thinks it's tempting," Sisko said. He grinned at her, leaning against the door hatch, his arms crossed. When she simply deactivated the antigrav unit, he added, "But then again, you're only Terran."

Startled, Seven met his eyes. Then she removed the antigrav unit.

As she passed by Sisko, he added, "Even if you do act like you're better than everyone else."

Seven knew her "cover" was slipping. That was because she had no cover. "As you said, I'm only Terran."

"Seven, that's not appropriate attire," Kira chided her.

Seven glanced down at her gray Cardassian uniform. Technically, she had no right to wear a Gul's uniform, but Kira had insisted. "You deemed this suitable for my public appearances."

"Yes, but tonight we're going to Risa! You must be more festive than *that*." Kira was swathed in sheer white fabric, encircling one shoulder and wrapping around her body in nearly transparent layers down to trail behind her feet. Seven was unsure what made the voile cling to her skin.

"Marani, put something together for Seven," Kira ordered. "In black, of course, to complement my white. And hurry or we'll be late for the beam-down."

Seven allowed Marani to dress her in a shiny black vest and short skirt. Her black boots with their spiked heels made her tower above Kira even more. But Kira clapped her hands, delighted with the transformation. "When we go to Risa, Seven, you'll officially serve as my slave. No Free-Terrans allowed on Risa!"

Seven knew the trip to Risa was going to be an ordeal she would simply have to endure. Ever since Kira had moved her entourage onto the Negh'Var, Seven had been losing influence over Kira. She was now denied much of her earlier autonomy, and was fast becoming just another one of Kira's slaves, with Marani resuming the preferred position. That was not the situation that Seven wanted to be in, but it would have to do for now.

When they transported to the pleasure planet, Seven found it difficult to absorb everything she saw. She had grown accustomed to the isolation of Kira's quarters. On Risa, life-forms of every description milled about the cavernous entertainment malls or strolled along the causeways. They saw palaces of pleasure where food, gaming, and sensual delights overflowed in every direction.

Their entourage numbered nearly twenty, including guards and slaves. The hosts immediately snapped their fingers and gave Kira, Troi, or Worf anything they admired. Several Terrans were kept busy running to and from the transporter pads, delivering things to the *Negh'Var.*

For the second time since the tour began, Seven found herself in close proximity to Deanna Troi. The Regent's companion wore a filmy white scarf embroidered with tiny violets wrapped over her hair and twined around her neck. Her violet dress was cut daringly low, but she seemed reserved in the midst of the manic laughter of the carousing hordes. Seven caught her eyes several times, yet she was not worried that the empath would be able to detect more than a vague impression that she was different. The only thing she had to fear was feeling fear. According to the Obsidian Order dossier on Deanna Troi, fear would alert her quicker than anything else.

Even as Seven's senses were overwhelmed and numbed by the stimulus, she began to notice the Terrans. Terrans were everywhere, serving people, carrying things, and darting purposefully through the crowds. She saw barely dressed slaves cleaning up spills on the floor, repairing the broken tiles in the mosaic ceiling, and even opening doors.

By the time their party made their way to the enormous stadium where the Klingon opera was being presented, Seven saw masses of Terrans. She had never seen so many of them before. On most planets, Terrans were kept out of sight in the camps and work colonies.

She tried to not look at them, repulsed by their weakness. But she couldn't help but be fascinated. Clearly they were not the finest life-forms the galaxy had to offer, with their soft, unformed faces, and hunched servile attitudes.

Kira kept pointing out Terrans that appealed to her, and she seemed invigorated by the number of slaves. Seven finally understood why Kira liked having Terrans around. They were inherently inferior. She could use them without having to respect their wishes or choices. She could do whatever she wanted with them.

Seven knew she was allowing Kira to caress her and order her about because she was following Enabran Tain's orders. But it made her feel . . . Terran. Now that she was on Risa, she was legally a slave.

When they reached the Klingon Opera House, their party was cleared from the stadium entrance to transport directly into the premier box. Several slaves were already there, prepared to do anything they requested. Curved cushioned benches lined the several tiers of the box, and their entourage quickly settled in.

The opera was just beginning with the opening battle of Tong Vey. Seven knew the story of *Sompek's Revenge,* yet she could hardly follow the narrative thread through the shifting lines of warriors, their ranks clashing and milling in the vast expanse of the stage. Then Tow'ga appeared as Sompek, a giant among the masses, standing ten stories high through the aid of holo-imagery. He began to sing.

Seven clapped her hands over her ears, trying to stifle the clamoring discords. A thousand voices joined in, and ten thousand more from the watching crowd, ranked in tiers around the mock battlefield. Seven looked closer, through the blood and makeshift Klingon masks, to see the Terrans posing as Sompek's battalions. They fought and killed each other in front of the cheering crowd.

The barrage threatened to overwhelm her. Seven was near the door to the box, and noticed it was propped open.

She slipped outside. The corridor was enclosed, blocking the view of the stage below. It was mostly used by slaves rushing up and down, popping in and out of the boxes. The open doors let in the raucous singing along with the screams, but it was relatively subdued compared to being inside the box.

Then right behind her, a deep voice ordered, *"You, come with me."*

A tall Orion was pointing directly at Seven.

She backed away shaking her head. "I belong in here—"

"Not anymore." The Orion jerked a thumb. "Bring that one, too."

Several burly Terrans were ushering along a couple of young slaves. "Yer needed in the pleasure pits," one of them told her. The other two slaves shuffled up the steps, their heads bent.

"No!" Seven exclaimed.

Amazed, the Terrans looked at her, their eyes curiously blank. Then one of them grabbed her arm and started pulling her up the stairs.

Seven called out, "Kira! Overseer! Help me!"

There was a roar from the boxes at something on stage, and "Sompek" raised his bellowing another notch. Seven struggled, landing a blow to the midsection of the Terran. As he let go, she whirled, smacking the other Terran across the jaw with her high-heeled boot.

She ran back down the steps to the box where Kira and the Regent were still calling out encouragement to Sompek's men. Seven was pursued by the Orion, but he stopped short at the sight of the Regent's banner. Seven met his eyes defiantly as he slowly withdrew. The Orion seemed puzzled by her resistance.

Kira said, "Hand me that bowl, Seven."

Seven's hands were shaking as she picked up the delicate crystal bowl mounded with a sweet confection. No one had noticed she was gone. She could have been hauled off to the pleasure pits and never seen the light of day again. Kira probably would have shrugged and left her behind as the *Negh'Var* continued on to the Sol sector. Even Enabran Tain would have a hard time finding her on Risa. Blond Terran, which blond Terran? Everyone knows that Terrans look alike. . . .

Shaking even harder, Seven sat down on a cushion, pulling her knees up to her chest. For the first time since Enabran Tain had taken her into the Obsidian Order, she felt as if she wasn't safe.

Chapter 4

B'ELANNA, INTENDANT OF Sol sector, had much better things to do than to show Kira Nerys the sights of Vulcan. Yet here she was, at Spock's shrine, a decrepit sphere balanced on a tiny fulcrum. The shrine had been created during the final days of the Terran Empire. The Alliance allowed it to remain standing, though they did nothing to stop the slow disintegration of the oxidizing metal. Klingons honored warriors fallen in combat regardless of which side they fought on, so B'Elanna had opposed stiff pressure from other Alliance members to topple the sphere and raze Spock's shrine to the ground.

Kira waved at an inscription. "Read it, Seven."

The blond Terran was wearing a brief slave's tunic, revealing her long legs. She calmly read the words incised under the image of a hand, the fingers spread in the V-shaped Vulcan greeting. *"Commander-in-Chief Spock transformed the Terran Empire with his message of reform, pressing for disarmament and peace. The galaxy will remember his unique contributions. Spock was killed during the battle of Mutara, facing the Alliance forces. 'Oh starless night of boundless black . . .' "*

"How . . . Vulcan," Kira said with a slightly upturned nose. "That's all they've got to say about the last Commander-in-Chief of the Terran Empire?"

"The empire was in rapid decline when they established this shrine," B'Elanna irritably reminded her. "But they diverted titanium to build it."

"Not very good quality titanium." Kira laughed, gesturing to the divots and holes in the plating of the sphere.

"The old mining methods were not as adept at generating pure titanium." B'Elanna shrugged.

"Fascinating . . ." Kira drawled in amusement.

"You said you wanted the tour!" B'Elanna retorted. "I'm ready to leave whenever you are."

"I want to stay," Kira replied, smiling blandly.

B'Elanna seethed inside. Blast Spock and the Vulcans, and blast Kira Nerys! She didn't want to be here in the searing heat, discussing history lessons. She should be assessing the mining production levels in the asteroid belt between Mars and Earth to adjust the export schedule. Mining on Earth had been halted again because of the release of toxins left in the soil by the old Alliance weapons. The last transport of mining slaves to the surface had been lost. But the scientists on Utopia Planitia were working on a way to crack Earth open to get to the mineral wealth inside. She had been forced to postpone an important science briefing in order to escort the new Overseer around Vulcan.

B'Elanna paced away from Kira and her entourage, ignoring the shafts of blinding light that slanted through the holes in the sphere. The metal was so hot that it radiated, making it warmer inside the sphere despite the shade. The tracery of titanium lines showed where the sphere was still structurally sound, but it appeared to be an illusion how it managed to balance on the fulcrum. B'Elanna had learned the meaning of that symbol during her first year as Intendant of Sol. A single person could move the galaxy.

Right now, Kira was the fulcrum, forcing everyone to move around her. B'Elanna was certain Kira had only requested this tour to aggravate her.

"You there, B'Elanna! Come over here," Kira ordered from across the sphere.

Gritting her teeth, B'Elanna flung her dark tail of hair over her shoulder. She wished she could draw her knife and fight Kira right on the spot. Instead, she strode over, facing Kira with her hands on her hips. "Now what?"

Kira gave her an offended look. "Is that how you talk to your Overseer?"

"What do you want?" B'Elanna demanded.

The slaves shifted uneasily as Kira stared at B'Elanna, tapping the toe of her boot against the sphere, making it ring. "I can see why the Terrans in this system don't know their place."

B'Elanna could feel several of her Klingon guards pressing closer behind her, taking offense at Kira's tone.

"How could they when the Terran in charge doesn't know *her* place?" Kira finished blandly.

B'Elanna felt her face flush red, and her hands clenched into fists. "I'm Klingon!"

Her shout echoed in the sphere, and she realized she was shaking. Kira was quietly chuckling, her hand raising to her mouth as if to conceal her amusement.

"This *tour* is over," B'Elanna said flatly.

"But you haven't heard what I wanted," Kira protested.

B'Elanna snapped, "What is it already!"

"I want those." She pointed toward two identical young Vulcans standing on either side of the arched entrance in the sphere.

"The Vulcan eunuchs?" B'Elanna asked. "They've been consecrated to the shrine since their birth."

"Not anymore," Kira said. "Now they belong to me."

This time B'Elanna laughed, a bitter taunting sound. "I think not!"

"Why you little upstart," Kira murmured in astonishment.

"Upstart!" B'Elanna snorted. "It wasn't me who was staffing a security desk in some backwater territory two years ago."

Kira blinked a few times, then got a look on her face like a gutter rat, pointed and fierce. "You'll do what I tell you."

"I do what the Alliance tells me," B'Elanna retorted.

"In this case, it's the same thing," Kira said darkly.

B'Elanna took a step closer, pleased that she was

taller than Kira and could lean into her face. "This tour is over. Go back to the *Negh'Var.*"

Kira glanced at the Klingon guards. Their arms were crossed and they were snarling because of the exchange.

"Those Vulcan eunuchs are mine," Kira said quietly. Then she turned and gathered her Terran slaves, leaving Spock's shrine with resounding steps that shook the sphere. She didn't even glance at the eunuchs as she passed between them.

"*HI'Qip!*" B'Elanna spat as the Bajoran left. Her Klingons grunted in agreement. B'Elanna was sick of this so-called Overseer and her greedy, overbearing ways. Her only consolation was that Kira was bound to ruin it for herself. Nobody could be that antagonistic and manage to survive.

B'Elanna returned to the Alliance headquarters on Vulcan, landing on top of the towering structure that faced the steep slope of Mount Surak. It was her command post in this system, on the far side of the Sol sector. As long as the Regent's flagship remained in orbit, she would have to stay in the Vulcan system, despite her pressing need to return to Sol.

The landing deck was busy with Klingon guards and militia. The Klingon community on Vulcan was mostly couples or triads with children. It was quieter than and relatively isolated from the interstellar traffic around the Sol system, in the heart of the sector. The administrators were Vulcans; slaves, in every sense of the word, who managed the business of the Sol sector. After B'Elanna found out how efficient and compliant the Vulcans were, she used them in all of her headquarters.

The Intendant's office on Vulcan offered a 180-degree view of the ruddy, smoking-hot plains at the base of Mount Surak. But B'Elanna had long since become used to the vista, ignoring it as she seated herself at the computer. "Get me the commander of the *Sitio.*"

The Klingon warrior in command of her starship soon appeared on the screen. Rugha was an older woman with penetrating eyes and grizzled hair and brows. B'Elanna trusted Rugha with her life.

"How long before the *Sitio* can leave orbit and return to Mars?" B'Elanna asked.

Commander Rugha clearly hadn't expected the request, but she replied, *"We can depart immediately, Intendant."*

"Fine, I'll be coming on board soon. B'Elanna out."

B'Elanna then called Worf, intending to request that they return to Utopia Planitia, where she had important business concerning Earth mining. She didn't intend to wait on Kira any longer. Surely Worf would grant her request.

However, Koloth, the first officer on the *Negh'Var,* replied that the Regent was in seclusion. B'Elanna submitted her request and signed off with a sigh. It was evening on the *Negh'Var,* and she wasn't sure when he would respond. She would have to get her schedule in synch with the *Negh'Var* as quickly as possible.

B'Elanna had not yet spoken to Troi since the armada had arrived, so she didn't know how the Betazoid was taking Kira's presence on the flagship. B'Elanna had suspected that Kira would try to win Worf's affections as a way to control the Regent. Funny how Worf hadn't seen it, even though Kira had made herself perfectly clear at the Alliance gathering.

In a contest of wills, B'Elanna decided she would back Troi any day. Troi knew the benefits of creating a good relationship with the people around her. B'Elanna's interactions with Troi were always mutually beneficial. That was the proper way to wield power.

Since B'Elanna didn't know how long it would take to hear from Worf, she settled in to do some work. First, as always, she checked on the progress of the Duras murder investigation. It was her last link to Duras, the man who had protected her for nearly two decades, counseling her and raising her up as Intendant of Sol. She still sometimes couldn't believe she would never drink bloodwine with him again.

Her team had determined that the energy signature left by the assassin was not Klingon in origin, nor was it typical of any particular alien species. Examples of bio-implants that emitted similar energy signatures were found in both the Alpha and Beta Quadrants. Since the Duras sentries hadn't taken a level-one source scan, B'Elanna couldn't pinpoint the origin.

In addition, there was nothing to be discovered in the way Duras had died. Except that B'Elanna agreed with Worf that Duras had not been killed by a Klingon. There was no honor in this death.

Now the investigators were trying to correlate evidence from Duras's death with other assassinations. As

B'Elanna ticked through the list of coincidences and unlikely associations, one suddenly stood out. The Bajoran First Minister, Winn Adami, had also been killed when an assassin snapped her neck.

Using the carte blanche Worf had given her with unlimited authority to gather what she needed during the investigation, B'Elanna obtained all of the information Bajoran officials had collected on the recent assassination of Winn Adami. They believed that Tora Ziyal, a Cardassian/Bajoran who had served as Winn's assistant, had been involved. Some believed Ziyal had killed Winn herself, generating vague suspicions against various Cardassian leaders.

But B'Elanna remembered the bitter fighting at the Alliance gathering when Winn Adami had tried to become the Bajoran Intendant. Kira had won, but Winn had kept control of Bajor itself. Now that Winn was dead, Kira had a free hand to do as she chose.

Kira had also benefited from the death of Duras. Worf had intended for Duras to fill the Overseer's post, but now Kira held it.

Though B'Elanna was nearly convinced of Kira's guilt, she only had circumstantial evidence. She instantly sent a message to her investigators, instructing them to research the possible connections between the death of the Bajoran First Minister and Duras. She dispatched a team to conduct her own interviews with Bajorans in the Ministry complex.

If Kira had anything to do with the death of Duras, B'Elanna would personally destroy her.

It was a pleasant daydream. What if she did crush Kira . . . the other Intendants would probably be so grateful they would support her bid for Overseer. B'Elanna had proven that it worked to have a half-Terran in charge of the Sol sector, so why not the former Terran Empire? Never had production and trade been higher in Sol, resulting in greater wealth for the other members of the Alliance.

But B'Elanna was too practical. She knew the Cardassians would never support an Overseer whose primary allegiance was Klingon.

When the blue light on her communications array flashed, B'Elanna immediately answered, hoping it would be Worf. Instead, it was the head of her personal guards. *"Intendant, there's been a disturbance at Spock's shrine. The Vulcan eunuchs were taken by Terran slaves. The shuttle bore the registry of the Negh'Var so the security team broke off pursuit."*

"No!" B'Elanna exclaimed. "That *joj'uSDu'!*"

The guard dryly added, *"The Overseer was not identified at the scene."*

B'Elanna made a frustrated sound in her throat. *"Obviously* that's who did it." She closed the connection, too furious to properly sign off. But it wasn't the guard's fault. It was that crazed Bajoran running amok. What arrogance, stealing the eunuchs from the shrine!

B'Elanna punched her emergency link directly to Worf. She had only used it a handful of times. But Kira was directly challenging her authority, and she wouldn't wait a nanosecond to stop her.

The screen remained gray for several heartbeats, until

Worf's head appeared. His hair was standing out wildly, and there was a long scratch near his mouth. When he spoke, she could see blood on his teeth, indicating he had been hit hard enough to break flesh.

"Who disturbs me!" he roared into the screen.

B'Elanna recognized the blood lust in his eyes, and his heavy-breathing focus on getting satisfaction. Over his shoulder, she could see a vague form with curling dark hair falling down her back. At least he wasn't with Kira.

"My apologies," B'Elanna said quickly. "But Kira has stolen two Vulcan eunuchs from the shrine—"

"You bother me about *'Iw-slaves!'* " Worf was already looking back at Troi, distracted from B'Elanna. She knew she only risked infuriating him by pressing it now.

"I have to return to Utopia Planitia immediately," B'Elanna told him instead, reverting to the original reason she had left a message for him. Later, she would recover the eunuchs. "I suggest you leave Kira on Vulcan if she wants more sight-seeing. But I need to work on the Earth deep-core mining—"

"Then do it," Worf interrupted.

"Shall I inform Koloth to accompany the *Sitio?*" B'Elanna asked, holding firm.

"Yes. Worf out."

The screen went black, and B'Elanna slammed both her fists into the top of the desk. Even when she was right, she was stifled at every turn!

But she swore, in the end, she would make Kira pay for this.

Chapter 5

THERE WAS NOTHING like Utopia Planitia anywhere in the galaxy. Kira Nerys thrilled to the decaying grandeur of the shipyards orbiting Mars, once the center of the infamous Terran Empire. The vast interlocking blocks of gridwork were in use, holding starships for repair. Sections of the grid had been removed and reattached as needed since the rise of the Alliance, and larger ships were nestled now in the skeleton frames. The space around Mars was busy, crisscrossed by tiny repair rovers and vessels of every size.

The *Negh'Var* was surrounded by open drydock scaffolding, held in place with large articulated work arms. The enormous warp coils were being refitted. Even restrained, the Alliance flagship was a commanding presence.

Worf refused to take quarters on the surface of Mars, preferring to remain on his ship. Kira shook her head ruefully when she heard about that, thoroughly enjoying her quarters in the opulent city of Utopia Planitia. Mars offered every conceivable pleasure in the Alliance, and it seemed as if everyone stopped by the Sol system. But Worf wasn't enjoying any of it. Finally she realized that it was because his flagship was in dock. It made him feel paralyzed, and he was spreading his discomfort to everyone.

Each day Kira was discovering more about Worf and his peculiar whims. He was definitely not easy to get along with. And while he seemed to enjoy her company and appreciate her humor, nothing more ever came of it.

Kira almost skipped the science briefing about deep-core mining taking place on B'Elanna's ship, figuring it would bore her. But when she found out that Deanna Troi would be joining Worf and B'Elanna, she changed her mind. After watching Troi so closely during the tour, Kira had come to believe the Betazoid knew when something was worth a closer look. Smart wasn't the word for Troi. She seemed always to ask the right questions to get to the very heart of the matter. So Kira got up early and transported to the *Sitio* rather than be left out of something important.

Before they were halfway through the science briefing on deep-core mining, Kira realized this experimental technology could yield an embarrassment of mineral wealth. They could double the Alliance fleet in ten standard years, offering tremendous strategic possibilities on the Romulan front. They could also build new space stations at five times the current rate, allowing the Alliance to control more territory. Kira intended to get a copy of the science briefing for her own people so they could start mining worthless hunks of metal, like the moon Jerrado, rather than tearing up the purple Bajoran mountainsides.

Kira yawned, leaning back in her chair, kicking one foot up on the oblong conference table. It was still boring. There was a cute holo-simulation of the planet Earth with lasers piercing the thin atmosphere, hitting a rolling sand plain. The ground exploded on contact. The view cut to a cross section of lasers boring through the rock layers to reach the mineral pockets beneath the crust. Tiny forms dropped on antigrav units from the lip of the completed shaft, as slaves guided the auto-miners in removing and transporting the material.

Kira reminded herself to mention this technology to Seven. Perhaps there was some way she could exploit it from her position as Overseer. Maybe a trade tax on all deep-mined material . . .

Meanwhile, her eyes wandered from Worf and the ever-attentive Troi to B'Elanna, sitting next to her. The half-Klingon frowned at Kira's raised boot smearing the mirror finish of the table, before turning her attention back to the woman narrating the presentation. The scientist was a Terran with lovely café coloring and a thick mane of black hair. Her trim gray uniform with the Sol symbol on her left shoulder indicated that she was a Free-Terran rather than a slave.

The striking Terran concluded the presentation with "Are there any questions?"

"Yes," Kira said instantly. "What is your name, my dear?"

"Dr. Jennifer Sisko," the woman said quietly, her hands clasped together below her waist.

"You came in late," B'Elanna dryly reminded Kira.

Kira ignored the surly Intendant. "Sisko? Why, I have a Terran named Sisko. Benjamin Sisko."

Jennifer bit her lip. "Ben . . . I heard he was in the Bajoran sector."

Eagerly, Kira sat forward. "Tall, dark and too sly for his own good? That Benjamin Sisko?"

"Yes," Jennifer admitted, getting herself under control. Her glance shifted to B'Elanna and the others.

"You're his wife," Kira said. "Aren't you?"

Jennifer's full lips compressed. "Ex-wife," she bit off.

B'Elanna slapped the top of the table with her palm. "Can we please have this family reunion some other time? This is supposed to be a science briefing."

Kira settled back, while Jennifer Sisko answered Deanna Troi's questions about sensor echoes and the difficulty of detecting explosive liquids from a planetary orbit.

Kira knew Benjamin had a wife, of course, from the investigation her security team had run on the Terran shortly after he showed up in Bajoran territory. She had forgotten her name was Jennifer until now. Whenever Kira had questioned Benjamin about his wife, he acted thankful to get away from her. Kira had imagined her to be a harridan and a hag, but this woman was exquisite!

The idea of taking Jennifer back to Bajor was simply

too delicious for words. It offered all sorts of wonderful possibilities for tormenting Benjamin.

Kira waited until Jennifer was dismissed by B'Elanna. The Terran avoided looking at Kira as she hurried from the briefing room, clutching her disks to her chest.

Kira turned to Worf, "I *must* have her! What a marvelous coincidence to find her here—"

"Not on your life!" B'Elanna shouted at Kira. "You keep your grubby hands off my people."

"Now, now," Kira warned her, "we already had this discussion. Look what happened last time."

"Yeah, you stole two Vulcan eunuchs from me!" B'Elanna stood up, facing Kira. "I want them back, *now.*"

Kira waved her off. "That has nothing to do with Jennifer Sisko." She smiled sweetly across the table at Worf. "Surely one Terran is of no consequence."

"Her sensor knowledge is essential to the deep-core mining project," B'Elanna protested. "Besides, she's a Free-Terran. You do understand the concept of 'Free-Terran'?"

"Of course," Kira said lightly. "My Sisko is a Free-Terran, and so is Seven. They're still only Terrans."

"Terrans run this sector," B'Elanna said grimly.

"Oh that's right . . . I keep forgetting you're Terran, too . . ."

B'Elanna leaned into her face, just like she'd done at Spock's shrine, only this time Worf and Deanna Troi were witnesses. "I'm *Klingon!*" B'Elanna shouted, spitting in her face.

"Stop*!*" Worf thundered, making both of them cringe.

B'Elanna drew back, but Kira gave her a push to hurry her up.

Worf's expression was dark. "You," he ordered B'Elanna, jabbing a finger at her, "be silent! And you," he said to Kira, "keep away from that Terran. She is needed here."

The Regent ponderously got to his feet, effectively ending the discussion. His hand swiped the wine from his mustaches. "I will return to the *Negh'Var* now."

Deanna half-rose from her seat, startled. "I thought we were going to the armada reception in Utopia Planitia."

"*Ghobe,*" Worf said flatly. He stalked out the door, not bothering to wait for his companion.

Troi sat back down at the table with a sigh. B'Elanna glared at Kira, before stalking after Worf. She was probably going to harass him about the Vulcan twins . . . just what he needed right now to improve his mood.

Kira slung one hip on the polished conference table, looking out the window at the glittering metallic mesh entangling the various starships. She surreptitiously examined Troi, wondering if the Betazoid was upset by Worf's abrupt behavior. Kira knew if Worf had treated her like that, she would want to destroy him and everything he loved.

But no matter what happened, Troi never reacted. That sigh was the first sign Kira had seen that she could get upset. Now, Troi simply gazed at the shipyards along with Kira, pensively accepting the inevitable. But somehow, instead of making her appear weak, she seemed stronger. A gossamer woman with an iron strength of will.

Kira's feigned curiosity in Deanna Troi was no longer feigned. It had been real for some time, as was her admiration for the sultry beauty. She rode the turbulence of politics with a style that Kira envied. She never seemed to let inconsequential people like B'Elanna get in her way.

"If Worf wants a Terran to be Intendant of Sol," Kira said ruefully, "my Seven would do a better job."

Troi laughed quietly. "Klingons are not known for holding their tempers. And B'Elanna has a lot on her mind. There's the big Alliance Celebration in a few days."

Kira raised one hand in token agreement. The celebration of the Alliance victory over the Terran Empire was drawing Intendants and high-ranking Alliance officials from far-flung sectors. Kira's slaves were creating a costume that was intended to bring everyone to their knees. It involved the Vulcan twins, whose sallow skin nicely complemented her red hair.

Kira silently vowed that, like the Vulcan eunuchs, Jennifer Sisko would be brought to Bajor. Soon. She didn't intend to let B'Elanna get the upper hand with her.

But now she was being offered a different sort of opportunity. "Do you still want to go to the reception?" Kira asked. "I'm beaming down myself."

Troi smiled. "We could go together."

Kira was pleased as they headed toward the turbolift. Her private goal for this tour had been to neutralize Troi as a threat. Since Worf was turning out to be uncooperative, she was open to alternative plans. Perhaps it would be best to win Troi over with her charms. It had worked with Seven, why not Deanna Troi?

Chapter 6

WHEN DEANNA TROI received the signal from the docking crew, she immediately went to the holosuites to find Worf. As usual, he was sparring with B'Elanna to pass the time. His temper had worsened while the refit of the *Negh'Var*'s warp coils was carried out.

Troi understood the strain Worf was under, so she had taken matters into her own hands, issuing orders and approving new work schedules. Now she would see if it was worth the resentment of the engineering crew, whose shore leave on Utopia Planitia she had canceled.

She waited until Worf and B'Elanna had finished their match. While they were still in their sweaty workout clothes, she urged them to follow her to the observation bay. Worf was so irritable that he almost refused, but his gaze rested on the excitement dancing in her smile, and he finally relented.

Troi urged B'Elanna to come when the Sol Intendant would have declined out of politeness. But Troi wanted to talk to B'Elanna before the Alliance Celebration. With the festivities scheduled to begin tomorrow morning, this could be her last chance.

Leading them both into the spacious observation bay, Troi was amused to see the Klingon crew members slip away when the Regent entered. Soon they were alone, standing close to the windowed hull. One of the enormous articulated arms of the drydock cut off the view, curving around the flagship to grip its bulbous bow.

Worf growled low in his throat, unpleasantly reminded of the *Negh'Var*'s immobility.

Troi hit her comm badge. "Docking crew, you can proceed."

Bullet-shaped tug ships darted in, with one streaking directly underneath the observation lounge. There was a pause; then the *Negh'Var* lurched slightly. The faint scream of metal scraping against metal echoed through the ship as the articulated arm began to move at the joints, pulling away from the observation window. There was a slight buoyancy in the deck as if the flagship was drifting. Then the small tug ships grabbed hold. The articulated arm was retreating faster now, with the pointed end moving clear of the *Negh'Var.*

"Your ship, Commander," Troi said with a half-bow and flourish toward the window.

"The refit is complete?" Worf asked in amazement.

She modestly shrugged. "I doubled the work crews."

With a roar of approval, Worf lifted her up and swung

her around. "My *Imzadi*," he said proudly, giving her a sound kiss on the lips. "My heart . . ."

Troi was glad that her surprise had worked. He rarely paid attention to repair reports, so he hadn't noticed that the refit was proceeding at nearly twice the pace he had expected.

"I must go to the bridge." There was a faraway look in his eyes, as if he was eager to set off for the stars again. Without another word, Worf leaped up the tiered steps three at a time.

Troi didn't mind his abrupt exit. It was enough to know that he was content.

"Whew!" B'Elanna exclaimed, throwing herself into the nearest seat. There was a cut on her chin and drops of blood splotched down the front of her gee. "You're the only one who can make him happy, Deanna."

"It was nothing," she murmured.

"He's been impossible to deal with," B'Elanna continued, fanning the sweat on her face and neck. "Every time we stopped to rest, he kept complaining about the refit. No matter how many times I explained that manufacture and repair is up a hundred and twenty-three percent!"

Troi had thought long and hard about how to draw Kira under her influence. The Bajoran was suspicious of everyone; charming on the surface, but letting nothing touch her deeply. Troi decided that B'Elanna could be useful in accelerating an intimacy between her and Kira.

Troi sat down next to B'Elanna. "I bet Kira is complaining about Sol sector."

"That *p'tok!*" B'Elanna spat out viciously. But she reclined back as if weary of Kira.

"Of all the Intendants, you've been the most resolute," Troi told her. "I've heard endless complaints, but then they always turn around and kiss her feet. I'm half expecting she'll make that her next official ritual. 'When one meets the Overseer, one must kiss her feet . . .' "

"I'd spit on them!" B'Elanna vowed.

"I think something will happen at the Alliance Celebration," Troi continued. "There's so many officials arriving . . . Kira will insist on taking precedence over everyone. Especially you because it's your sector."

B'Elanna shifted in her seat as if she wanted to hit something. "Worf should stop her."

"Worf will not speak to me about Kira," Troi said regretfully. "But I think Kira abuses her position. She provokes us to humiliate us."

Frustrated, B'Elanna thrust herself from her chair, pacing back and forth in front of the window. "Somebody has to stop her."

Troi knew truer words had never been spoken. "Somebody should at least try. I know I won't be handing over national treasures when we reach Betazed."

Troi could tell by B'Elanna's inner turmoil that her words were having the desired effect. The Sol Intendant was fidgeting and biting her lip.

"Oh, well. Everyone's afraid of her." Troi sighed as she turned away. "I better get to the bridge and make sure Worf is happy." She didn't want to resolve anything with B'Elanna, preferring to leave her in a heightened, sensitized state. Surely B'Elanna wouldn't have the self-restraint to stay away from Kira during the party, and Kira would inevitably do something obnoxious. Troi would be prepared to take advantage of whatever arose. "I'll see you tomorrow at the Alliance Celebration."

Distracted, B'Elanna hardly bid her good-bye, still fuming over Kira Nerys.

Troi went to the bridge to make sure Worf was back in command mode. With all of these important people coming to the Alliance Celebration, it was imperative that Worf be in the right frame of mind. Now, as an extra bonus, he would be willing to give her anything she asked for.

Troi was quite satisfied with her afternoon's work. Most people didn't realize how important it was to prepare for large events such as these.

When Troi and Worf transported onto the party barge, it looked like any other Alliance gathering. Many of the key players were there, including Natima Lang, head of the Cardassian Detapa Council, and the Intendants from Orion, Breen, Tholia, Trill, and other far-flung empires. They each had numerous attendants and slaves accompanying them.

Troi credited the presence of a number of high-ranking officials to Kira's heavy-handed methods. Who would pass up an opportunity to network with other disgruntled leaders?

Accompanied only by Keiko, Troi completed her

business early. Most important was the consignment deal with the gracious Orion Intendant, Varinna. Varinna guaranteed her the pick of the creches, insuring that plenty of animal women would be available at New Hope. Troi also settled her deal with the Tholian government for the manufacture and maintenance of new holo-simulators. A few more details, and she would have everything in place for the success of New Hope. Everything except for the necessary and lucrative gaming licenses.

Before boarding the party barge, Troi had carefully erected her mental blocks as she always did in preparation for crowds. But she could clearly sense the unrest in the large bubble as it cruised through space toward the planet Earth. The tiered seating and rounded glass offered a view in almost every direction, including down. Only the very core was opaque, concealing the impulse engines of the barge.

Though they had long since left Utopia Planitia, people were still arriving, beaming onto the barge directly from their starships. Sparkling lights in the distance marked the battleships of the Alliance Armada, protecting the barge on its leisurely cruise.

The passing asteroid ring momentarily drew everyone's attention. The mining droids and tiny augmented personnel modules swarmed through the dangerous field of spinning asteroids. But when the mineral wealth was left behind, the voices returned to discontented murmuring as the various aliens grouped and regrouped on the steep round tiers. Plenty of black, star-studded sofas and chairs gave them niches to establish temporary fiefdoms.

B'Elanna rushed by once or twice, tending to the many details of running the party barge and preparing for the reenactment of the destruction of Earth by the Alliance. It was carefully orchestrated for the pleasure of the gathered dignitaries, and Troi hoped for B'Elanna's sake that the show was a success.

The party was in full swing when Kira finally arrived. Troi knew immediately because a ripple of anticipation ran around the space barge. The voices grew louder, and the music rose to compensate. Now it sounded like a real party, but Troi could tell that nervous energy was fueling it. It was not a healthy release of tension. Instead, the frustration and discontent seemed to build.

When she saw Kira, she could understand why everyone was reacting in such a primal way. Kira wore a mesh of emeralds and blue-green sapphires clinging to her bare skin. The unique design revealed rather than concealed her body. Even more striking was the long green cape that hung from her shoulders, liberally embroidered with emeralds and studded with Greorian diamonds. The entire outfit was worth more than most Intendants acquired during a standard year.

The costly cloak was held up by two slender Vulcan youths, wearing only dark green loincloths. They followed Kira, staying several paces behind to display the intricate workmanship on the cloak. Troi pursed her lips, wondering if this was the project Kira's slaves had been working on for the past week. They all wore green loincloths and were lightly sprinkled with jewels. They cleared a path in front of Kira to prevent supplicants from getting too close.

Kira paused here and there to greet various Intendants and their guests, but she seemed preoccupied with the hundreds of eyes following her every movement. She was euphoric from the attention, glittering in wealth and adulation.

Troi resumed her seat, watching Earth grow from a fist-sized ball to the size of a dinner plate. Worf was somewhere down below on the see-through floor, among a dark group of Klingon warriors. As usual, they did honor to the gathering by wearing their worn and stained battle armor.

Troi had chosen to be unobtrusive in a black velvet sheath dress that was slit up one leg to her hip. The silver net that held her hair was fitted with tiny antigrav units, floating the curls back from her face in a sparkling cloud. After seeing Kira's outfit, she was glad she had restrained herself. Kira would have resented any competition.

When Kira finally circled up to her level, she gave Troi the once-over, then winked. "Perfect as always, my dear."

"Thank you, but you've outdone us all." Troi inclined her head, speaking only for Kira. The near-naked slaves maintained a buffer zone around the Overseer, allowing only those whom Kira acknowledged to come near.

Kira paused, appreciating Troi's vantage point. They could see almost the entire barge from here.

Troi sensed a stab of anger before she knew where it came from. B'Elanna was a few tiers below, glaring up at Kira. The irate Klingon in full armor made straight for the Overseer, bristling and ready for battle. Troi was not sure what had caused such a violent reaction.

"Those are *my* Vulcans," B'Elanna called out in a ringing voice. "Give them back to me."

Kira slowly turned to look down on B'Elanna. She spoke for the benefit of the watching dignitaries. "Is that any way to speak to your Overseer?"

B'Elanna spat to one side, showing her contempt for Kira as she stepped onto the upper tier. Her fists were planted on her hips, emphasizing her polished *d'k tahg*. "Hand over those Vulcans."

"Ridiculous." Kira gave an airy wave behind her. The Vulcans stood impassively, as if unaware that they were the topic of discussion. "Who would carry my cape?"

B'Elanna shook with fury. She had spoken loud enough to attract attention, and now everyone was watching the argument. They stood eye-to-eye, neither of them backing down.

Troi carefully seated herself again to distance herself from the fray. It was perfect! Maybe B'Elanna would kill Kira, then everything would be solved. . . .

Instead, B'Elanna turned to her Klingon guards. "Set the shields to prevent these Vulcans from leaving." Then she turned to Kira with a sardonic smile. "Since they are essential to your costume, you may use them until we return to Utopia Planitia. But they stay with me."

Kira's surge of fury was detected only by Troi. "You will regret this," she said quietly.

B'Elanna was elated at having beaten her. "Now, if

you'll excuse me, I have to tend to the destruction of Earth."

Already a ripple of interest was stirring the crowd, as the guests turned to the rapidly approaching planet. The vivid blue arc blocked out a quarter of the starfield, and they were close enough to see the murky brown streaks amid the white swirling clouds. Dust from the orbital bombardment still hung in the atmosphere after several generations.

Starships were darting into place, subduing the "Terran resistance force" sent up from Earth. Troi knew the story, as did everyone in the Alliance. She had also seen the reenactment several times, so she wasn't distracted by the brilliant explosions.

Kira remained standing near her, apparently watching the display. But Troi could sense her inner turmoil as she fumed over B'Elanna. Troi knew it wasn't the two skinny slaves who concerned her. If B'Elanna succeeded in publicly taking back her Vulcans, it would deliver a severe blow to Kira's ego and status. Other Intendants would begin to resist her demands, and her structure of terror and intimidation could erode.

Troi joined Kira. Keiko stayed back with Kira's slaves.

"You want the Vulcans, don't you?" Troi asked softly.

Kira bit her lip. "They're a perfectly matched set. And they're divine bath attendants." Her tone grew imploring. "I can't bear to part with them."

Troi smiled. "Let me see what I can do."

Kira's eyes opened wider. "Would you? That would be wonderful. . . ."

Troi concealed her pleasure. Now Kira was frantically wondering why Troi had offered to help, especially since it would publicly humiliate her friend B'Elanna.

Kira's suspicions grew, along with her doubts. "I don't think B'Elanna will listen to reason."

"We'll see about that," Troi assured her. With a final squeeze of Kira's arm, she smoothly glided away. With only Keiko attending her, it was simple to disappear into the crowd.

Later, when she was sure Kira was distracted, Troi spoke to Worf. It was not difficult to convince him that his own power rested on the obedience of the Intendants. If they got in the habit of disobeying the Overseer, it was a short step to rebelling against the Regent. Worf was in such a good humor that he simply patted her cheek, and assured her that he would tell B'Elanna to let Kira have the Vulcan twins.

Much later, when the barge returned to the red planet of Mars, Kira made a big show of leaving with all of her slaves—including the Vulcan twins. B'Elanna openly scowled, unable to conceal her resentment over the Vulcans. Meanwhile, Troi was rewarded with a brilliant smile from Kira, and her whispered appreciation. "You are a marvel, Deanna. . . ."

Then Kira called out to B'Elanna, for all to hear, "Thank you for a lovely evening!"

As her party beamed off the barge, everyone began talking. Troi knew that the rumors would spread before morning. They would say that Kira was able to bend any Intendant to her will.

Troi would have preferred it if B'Elanna had killed Kira. But she was accustomed to making do with what was at hand. Now Kira was in her debt. It would be a very short step to gaining her complete confidence. Soon, Troi would have everything she needed to make New Hope a safe haven for the rest of her life.

Chapter 7

MANY YEARS AGO, Enabran Tain had placed an undercover Obsidian Order agent among Natima Lang's personal aides, anticipating the day when Lang might possibly sit on the Detapa Council. His foresight was being rewarded now. He was able to track Lang's activities, and influence her decisions through this trusted aide.

Tain had ordered the agent to encourage Lang to attend the Alliance Celebration in defiance of Ghemor's faction of the Detapa Council. Ghemor thought Cardassia should boycott Alliance events until their empire held a position of equal power. Tain's plan to remove Lang as the Head of the Detapa Council was progressing. Never in the history of Lang's reign had more people spoken out against her.

Tain also received the bonus of a detailed report about the Alliance Celebration from his agent in Lang's entourage. The agent had seen Seven, and had managed to pass her an emergency beacon. The other half was activated in Tain's fusion unit, waiting for Seven to open the channel.

It was essential that Tain speak to Seven. She had been out of touch since Kira had abruptly left on her grand tour. After their last conversation, Tain had thoroughly analyzed Seven's response patterns from the emotigraph and found something highly disturbing. Seven was experiencing personality flux.

The Obsidian Order had trained Seven carefully in order to prevent her conscience from interfering in her duties. Tain had rarely seen his methods fail, and he was astonished to find signs of weakness in Seven, of all agents. Yet her personality index was clearly fluctuating, almost as if she had returned to an adolescent state.

Tain had two theories for why this was happening: Seven had fallen in love, likely with Kira Nerys, or she was having a negative reaction to her Terran cover.

If Seven had indeed become attached to Kira, then her loyalties were temporarily divided, resulting in this current state of self-examination. But that was easily fixed. Tain could say the correct code-word sequence to trigger Seven's implant to emit a reconditioning pulse. She would still feel attraction to Kira, but her priorities would be corrected. Tain had reconditioned hundreds of agents before, and would do it hundreds of times in the future. There was no preventing these irrational impulses from rising from time to time. The treatment was always effective.

However, if Seven was bothered by her Terran cover, then that would require a slightly more nuanced approach. He had everything in place to proceed down that path if necessary.

Meanwhile, he replayed his agent's report on the Alliance Celebration, noting that the adjectives "subservient" and "obedient" were used to describe Seven. She had worn nothing but a green loincloth and sparkling body paint. Apparently she was faithfully performing her role as Kira's Terran slave. There had been no opportunity for the agent to speak to her, but they exchanged recognition signals and he had passed her the emergency beacon.

The fusion unit signaled, and Tain felt a stirring of real interest. It had been so long since he had faced a challenge. Even Gul Dukat was proving to be of little consequence. But he would deal with that later. . . .

Seven's voice was hushed. *"Agent Seven here."*

At the signal, the computer emotigraph program automatically activated. The personality index parameters were enhanced, and Seven's levels showed an increase in hormone and adrenal release.

"Report," Tain ordered, as usual.

"Kira possesses an ancient device that allowed me to instantly teleport into the Bajoran Ministry complex in order to kill Winn Adami."

"Elaborate," Tain ordered. Yet he also noted the emotigraph readout, indicating that Seven regretted killing Winn Adami. Tain wasn't sure which bit of information was more surprising.

"My implant contains an image of the portal. It is ca-

pable of bypassing high-level security fields." Seven went on to minutely describe the handheld device, as well as the sensation of falling and her instantaneous arrival.

"Is the portal accessible?" Tain asked.

"Its current location is unknown," Seven replied. *"It could be on Terok Nor, on the* Siren's Song, *or here in our quarters on the* Negh'Var."

From her description, the portal must be some kind of portable transporter with unique properties. Both times Seven had transported from orbit to the surface of Bajor. Tain was intrigued by its ability to pierce security systems, but her core mission had a higher priority. "What is your current situation?"

"Tensions are escalating," Seven replied. *"Kira and B'Elanna engaged in a public altercation at the Alliance Celebration over a pair of slaves. Kira ultimately took them despite B'Elanna's insistence that they be returned."*

Tain noted that Seven emphasized the role the slaves played. However, in his opinion, the cause of the altercation was unimportant.

"What about Kira's interactions with Deanna Troi?" Tain asked.

"Kira's behavior is typically inconsistent." Seven's disdain for Kira was clear.

Probing deeper, Tain asked, "Why hasn't Kira revealed that Troi tried to have her killed?"

"Unknown," Seven said briefly. *"I believe Kira could order me to kill Troi or B'Elanna using the portal."*

The personality index spiked abruptly, indicating her profound reluctance to do so.

"Have you associated much with Troi or B'Elanna?" Tain wished he could see her face. Her expression would tell him far more than the emotigraph.

"Negative. Kira orders the slaves to remain in our quarters. I have spoken to no one for days."

Tain rubbed his hand over his mouth, considering his options. Clearly Seven was disturbed by her Terran cover. He had not anticipated this, but perhaps it was a result of her Terran heritage. They were an inherently weak species, and posing as one could make Seven doubt herself. However, Tain knew she was Cardassian at heart. He had molded her, and he could make her do whatever he wanted.

"The current situation is too volatile for an assassination. You can not be involved if Kira proceeds." Tain knew Seven would probably be unable to perform such a mission in her current state. "You will refuse to kill anyone, and if necessary, extract yourself and return to the debriefing point."

"Acknowledged." There was a hint of relief in her voice.

"For now, you must make contacts among the Alliance officials. You're no use to me hidden away."

"But I am . . . Terran." Seven sounded at a loss. *"That is, my cover is Terran. No one speaks to us."*

Tain smiled. "I've taken care of that. Remember you were raised Cardassian. I've arranged for your foster father to contact Kira Nerys and urge her to care for you properly."

"Ghemor?" Seven blurted out, her customary reserve shattered. *"He will help me?"*

"He has no choice," Tain said.

Seven was silent, and Tain again wished he could see her expression. Her anxiety and flight/fight response index were rising higher.

"I do not understand the objective . . ." Seven finally admitted.

Tain wished this were a problem that could be solved by simply triggering the deprogramming sequence that could eradicate any form of emotional attachment. However, a fundamental crack in Seven's core personality would need something special in order to be repaired.

"Seven, I want you to position yourself as a Cardassian instead of a Terran. I've decided that since your background has been exposed, we must use this opportunity. Few Cardassians are willing to venture outside our empire. We are too xenophobic for our own good. So the Klingons are spreading throughout the fallen Terran Empire, while we are losing ground. You're perfectly placed to network with Alliance officials, and backed by Ghemor, whose faction is strong on the Detapa Council, you could become an Alliance official. A sector inspector perhaps. Perhaps even an Intendant. We must have other alternatives than Gul Dukat . . ." Tain finished bitterly.

The truth seemed to calm Agent Seven. *"I see."*

"Maintain your connection with Kira, but not as a slave," Tain ordered. "That should make it easier to catch the attention of Alliance officials."

"Indeed," Seven agreed, her composure once more in

place. *"They will believe I have influence with the Overseer."*

Tain reminded her, "If you must extract yourself, locate the portal and take it with you. A device that can circumvent security systems should not stay in Kira's hands."

"Understood," Seven acknowledged. The emotigraph stayed steady.

Tain was satisfied that he had placed Seven back on track. Now was the time to clinch his hold over her. His voice lowered confidentially, as warm and loving as he could make it. "I'm sure you'll make me proud, Seven."

Seven hesitated. *"Thank you for this opportunity. And your confidence in me."*

Tain shut down the fission unit after Seven signed off. It was done. Seven's frustrations with appearing Terran would be assuaged by positioning herself as a Cardassian. Now she would be preoccupied with seeking a high office in the Alliance. With a clear goal in sight, Seven would always stay right on track.

Seven's call had been perfectly timed. Tain had planned to venture out of the Obsidian Order bunker that evening for the second time in only a handful of months. Few people knew where the headquarters were located, and Tain preferred to keep it that way. The fact that Gul Dukat had found the bunker infuriated him. Dukat had become too powerful to be safely ignored.

But Tain finally had the advantage. The genetic tissue samples had confirmed his suspicion. Ziyal was the daughter of Dukat and the Bajoran woman Tora Naprem. Tain had ordered Ziyal to be seized and brought to Cardassia Prime. Her kidnapping had fortunately coincided with the assassination of Winn Adami, bringing suspicion against Ziyal.

Two agents met him at the deep-level car bay to hand over custody of Tora Ziyal. The enveloping Bajoran robe and skull cap looked absurd with her Cardassian features. Tain had ordered that she be dressed in her own clothes, and he approved of the incongruous result.

Tain had delayed presenting Ziyal to her father in order to fan the flames against her. On Bajor, it was now commonly believed that Ziyal had murdered her beloved mentor, Winn Adami. Her ingrained Cardassian nature was blamed, and many were suspicious that she was a spy and assassin who had been planted in Winn's household as a foster child.

Tain didn't care about Cardassia's strained relations with Bajor. It was enough that Ziyal could never go home. He wanted her on Cardassia Prime causing embarrassment for Dukat. There was no way Dukat could live down fathering a half-Bajoran woman who was accused of murdering the First Minister of the neighboring territory.

"You again!" Ziyal exclaimed when she saw Tain. "Let me go! When my people find out what you've done to me—"

"Your people are Cardassian," Tain reminded her.

"My mother was Bajoran!" Ziyal protested. She clutched her ministerial garments closer as if to assure herself of that.

"Don't let that little wrinkle in your nose fool you," Tain told her. "You're more Cardassian than you know."

He locked her into the back of the ground car and took his seat in the front, next to the driver. "Did you watch those programs I sent?"

Ziyal pressed her thin lips together, turning her face away. Tain had provided her with Bajoran media reports proclaiming her guilt in the assassination of Winn Adami.

"All the evidence points to you, Tora Ziyal." Tain watched her as the car lifted vertically out of the launch tube. Three other cars joined them, two above and one below, carrying agents who would guard Tain on this rare outing. It would take them several minutes to reach the top access port of the bunker.

"You killed her!" Ziyal shouted, beating on the glass between them with her fists. "I'll tell them everything. How you brought me here and kept me locked up."

"Your untimely departure was a coincidence," Tain said. "I care nothing about Winn's death. This is about your father."

"I don't believe you." Ziyal was shaking, she was so upset. Tain examined the computer display, noting her increased heart rate and breathing. She was a young woman, inexperienced at containing her emotional outbursts.

It sickened him the way she looked like Dukat. Her ridges were undefined, nearly disappearing along her jawline. And her wrinkled nose was offensive, as was the Bajoran earring. But at times, when she lifted her chin trying to be resolute, or when she jerked her head away, he could see Dukat in her.

Tain took satisfaction in holding Ziyal. He could topple his greatest foe by lifting a finger. That had given him much pleasure as he had planned the perfect denouement. He knew he must see it happen.

Tain had concluded, after Ziyal was interrogated several times, that she didn't know who her father was. Her mother, Naprem, must have thought it was safer to keep her child ignorant and far away from Cardassian politics. She had been smart. Dukat had several enemies who would love to be in Tain's position now, holding Dukat's life in his hands. Dukat was apparently not aware he had a half-Bajoran daughter, otherwise he would have taken more care to insure that she never came to Cardassia Prime.

Tain input his security code and the accessway opened above them. The first two cars performed a security sweep. They would make sure that no unwarranted attention was being paid to this particular spot in the rugged foothills of the Hebitian mountain range.

Soon the cars were skimming over the hilltops toward Cardassia City. Layers of mauve and gray clouds lowered over the distant spires and hooked-top towers of the capitol. The river gleamed silvery pink in the dying light, cutting a swath through the silhouetted buildings.

Tain wished he were back underground in the Obsidian Order bunker, but he needed an audience when he presented Ziyal to Dukat. Otherwise Dukat could try to hide Ziyal, or kill her, to rid himself of the embarrassment.

Ziyal pressed against the window in the back, soaking up the glorious sights of the passing city. She had never seen Cardassia before, and was more subdued now. As the car sank toward the grand assembly hall, avoiding the dramatic re-curve hooks lit by the sinking sun, she asked, "Are you taking me to my father?"

"Yes." Tain thought it would be better for her to know. He didn't want her to act surprised. "His name is Gul Dukat."

Ziyal looked disturbed. "I've heard of him. He was the last Intendant of Bajor, after Opaka died."

"Yes, Dukat is one of our military leaders. He met your mother at the Jerom Beta mining camp when he was the Alliance inspector of Terran slave compounds."

"How do you know?" Ziyal demanded.

"Your genetic sequence matches."

Tain's driver landed the car, waiting until the other three cars had joined them. As the canopy of the private hangar closed, the agents got into defensive positions. The hangar had been covertly leased, but the Obsidian Order took no chances.

Tain released the back door to let Ziyal out of the car. He no longer needed to hold her arm to make her follow him. The agents spread out in front and behind, keeping everyone away as they proceeded down the ramp into the round assembly hall. Her robes made a slight swishing sound as she walked.

The Stellar Ball was the annual celebration of the military elite. The number of uniforms was staggering, with too many milling officers filling the great round chamber. Tain muttered an order to one of the agents to find Dukat. He wasn't accustomed to sorting through so many people at once.

Ziyal looked frightened, and she was drawing a great deal of attention. Her garish robes practically assaulted the eyes, and her face was startling with its odd mixture of Cardassian and Bajoran features. Soon people were pointing and staring.

The agent finally indicated a doorway where Dukat had appeared. Tain waited until Dukat entered the hall before carefully leading Ziyal to intercept him. Long before they reached one another, Dukat locked eyes with Tain.

There were several others with Dukat, including a white-haired dignified matron. That would be Dukat's wife, accompanied by favored wives of various lesser-ranking officers.

The attendees of the Stellar Ball pulled back to give them room to pass. The clamor fell hushed, becoming a continuous questioning murmur as the rest of the crowd turned to see what was happening.

Tain paused a few paces away from Dukat, making a sweeping gesture to Ziyal. "Dukat, may I present your daughter."

A gasp and a shriek rose from the other two women. Dukat's wife didn't react, she merely gazed at her husband, clutching her fan.

Dukat's face darkened in fury, his fist shaking at Tain. As Dukat advanced, several Obsidian Order agents inserted themselves between Dukat and Tain. "You slanderer!" Dukat exclaimed. "First you kill my father—"

"Your father was arrested and executed under the Cardassian system of justice," Tain interrupted, publicly setting the record straight. "Surely you recognize your own daughter, *Tora* Ziyal," he added, emphasizing her family name. "Though I'm sure it's been a while since you've seen Naprem, the young woman's mother."

Dukat hesitated as the realization of the truth came over him. His fist dropped, an unmistakable admission of guilt. Then he denied, "You lie, as you've always lied, Tain!"

Tain was pleased. Dukat was not nearly as certain now. Everyone could tell he was shaken. Ziyal was looking imploringly at Dukat, examining his face as if trying to understand. "Father?" she asked tentatively.

Dukat seemed struck to the very heart, breathing heavily and unable to move.

Tain nodded to his agents, who began handing small data rods to those who were closest. One agent went to Dukat's entourage, offering the rods. Dukat's wife steadfastly refused to accept one.

"You'll find the evidence on this data rod. Ziyal's genetic profile along with Gul Dukat's and the Bajoran woman, Naprem. You can test Ziyal yourself," Tain offered, most pleased with this last twist. "I want nothing more to do with her."

Tain turned and walked away, leaving Ziyal stranded on the floor of the assembly hall. Forcing Dukat to deal with her somehow. When he looked back from the steps, there was still a wide circle around Dukat and Ziyal.

Chapter 8

WORF REFUSED TO see B'Elanna for several days after the Alliance Celebration. She would be unable to curb her resentment about his order to relinquish the Vulcans. He would rather wait until she had exploded at some lesser official. Not that he minded smashing people flat with one blow, but B'Elanna deserved respect because she had been mentored by his most trusted friend, Duras.

This Kira business was growing tiresome. Everyone complained about her, begging for him to intercede. They had chosen Kira. They should shut up and deal with the consequences!

Only his *Imzadi* seemed immune, lifting herself above the stupid bickering. Though Kira had occasionally provoked her, Deanna remained gracious and polite. He knew she was anxious about those gaming licenses for her New Hope resort, and he fully intended she would get them. But he would do it in his own way.

As for Kira, he would put her down only if it was necessary—if she grew cocky toward him. She served a most unexpected and useful purpose by attracting criticism. In addition, his status had soared because she had lifted herself so high.

Now that the *Negh'Var* was released from the scaffolding, he made the hop from Mars to Jupiter Station for his annual inspection. The double-spindle station was dwarfed by the orange-striped gas giant. The *Negh'Var* went into synchronous orbit with the station, near the *Sitio*. When Worf and Kira beamed down, B'Elanna was waiting for them.

Worf enjoyed inspections, checking systems and personnel to be sure they were in excellent condition. He roared through Jupiter Station, determined that they would never forget a moment they had spent with the Regent. It took an iron fist to rule such a vast empire. That was why the Terrans had lost it.

By the time the inspection was over, Worf was feeling quite refreshed. B'Elanna accompanied him back to the *Negh'Var*, while Kira stayed on Jupiter Station to take the "cultural tour" of the Terran outpost, established over three centuries ago.

When they returned to Worf's quarters, B'Elanna seated herself with the vivid stripes of Jupiter filling the windows behind her. Worf was taking a deep swig of Trakian ale when B'Elanna started, "Worf, something must be done about Kira—"

Worf spat out the mouthful of ale, showering B'Elanna and the sofa. *"TammoH!"* he bellowed, all the more irritated because it was unexpected. He had forgotten about the incident with the Vulcan eunuchs. *"I* give the orders, not you!"

B'Elanna was dripping with silvery Trakian ale, but she glared up at him. "Kira's out of control! Did you see what she did to the manager of Jupiter Station? She's sending his best holo-engineer to Bajor to work on her holosuites! She can't go around doing that."

Worf was infuriated that B'Elanna wouldn't back down. Even when he leaned over her brandishing the ale flagon in one hand and his other fist nearly in her face, she continued to harp about Kira.

He either had to hit her or laugh about it. So he laughed, deep and satisfying. Then he called for more Trakian ale, having spilled most of his. Grelda scurried around, cleaning up. B'Elanna was looking wet and confused, as well she should.

"You think small." Worf lowered himself into his chair again. "Forget Kira. Soon she will no longer be a concern. The freer hand she is given, the quicker that day will come."

"You think someone will kill her?" B'Elanna asked.

Worf shrugged, as if it was a given. "Her security is lax."

"Maybe . . . but she's living on the *Negh'Var,*" B'Elanna pointed out. "No one will touch her on your flagship."

"Exactly!" Worf grinned, showing his teeth. "The power of the Overseer is nothing without the Regent."

They were interrupted by Grelda, who knew better than to disturb Worf unless it was dire. But Grelda indicated that an important message had just been relayed from the bridge.

Worf leaped up and strode to the computer terminal. Frowning, he opened the sealed message. It was from a most unexpected person—Gowron.

B'Elanna joined him, making a sound of distaste in her throat. Worf focused on the Klingon, knowing something momentous had occurred.

Gowron's bulging eyes were staring intently into the screen. *"Worf, we have not always been friends, but now is the time to place our animosity behind us. For the good of the Klingon Empire, for the good of the Alliance. Come back to Qo'noS. K'mpec is dead."* Gowron's face twisted in disgust. *"Died in his sleep. Come back to Qo'noS, Worf, and united we will stand strong for all Klingons."*

Gowron's sneer faded as the screen went black.

"K'mpec dead!" B'Elanna exclaimed in surprise. "I can't believe it. Do you really think he died in his sleep?"

"I have no doubt . . . the worthless old man."

"I bet Gowron wants your help to become Chancellor of the Klingon High Council." B'Elanna seemed doubtful. "How could he ask you after fighting against you all these years?"

"It is the Klingon way." Worf checked the *Negh'Var*'s

status to see how soon he could leave. He had Deanna to thank for completing the refit so fast.

"I'm not so sure," B'Elanna cautioned. "We can work with despicable life-forms, like the Cardassians, when it benefits the Klingon Empire. But how can you help Gowron after everything he's done to you?"

"The best alliances are often formed between enemies." Worf didn't foresee any problem in cooperating with Gowron. Besides, his feud had always been with K'mpec, not his protégé. Worf could think of no other warrior fit for the Chancellor's chair now that Duras was dead. Worf had never desired the post for himself; he preferred to remain free. "I must return to Qo'noS. I yearn to push a pain stick into the old man."

"You're leaving *now?*" B'Elanna asked.

"Yes. The armada will accompany me back to Qo'noS to witness the rites of succession." He glanced at B'Elanna. "The Overseer will no longer have the protection of the *Negh'Var.*"

"You're going to send Kira back to Bajor in her own cruiser?" B'Elanna's eyes widened at what that meant. "Oh . . . I wouldn't want to be on that voyage . . ."

Worf set aside the empty flagon. "The *Negh'Var* will depart in two hours."

Worf gave the orders to prepare for departure, then told Kira that the *Siren's Song* must be launched immediately. He cut off her questions, knowing everyone would receive Gowron's official announcement soon enough. First Officer Koloth would make sure the

Siren's Song was out of the vast launching bay before they departed.

Then he went to Deanna's quarters to tell her about the change in plans. She instantly recognized the advantages this would give Worf, especially from Gowron's proposed alliance. She affirmed again that she had never sensed devious feelings from Gowron toward Worf.

But she was not happy about leaving for Qo'noS. "It's too bad," she said wistfully. "I've been looking forward to getting back to Betazed II. There are some details waiting for my approval before the next stage can begin."

Worf slipped his arm around her shoulders, holding her close. "I will take you there first."

She started to smile, giving him a slight shove. "It's nearly a week in the other direction. By the time you get to Qo'noS, K'empec will be all shriveled up. No . . . you can't take me to Betazed."

"Perhaps B'Elanna can." Worf was enjoying the feel of her body against his. "As soon as Kira leaves Sol, she will be free to go."

"Kira might offer to take me," Deanna suggested.

"No!" Worf's arms tightened around her. "Promise me, you will not travel on Kira's ship. It is too dangerous. She has many enemies."

Deanna raised her brows slightly. "You have a point. I'll ask B'Elanna then . . . unless you'll miss me too much?"

Worf gently bit her cheek, savoring the firm, fragrant flesh. "I shall miss you. But you must go to your planet with the purple sky. I understand."

"Meanwhile . . . how long did you say we have?" She pushed him harder this time, making him stagger off balance.

Worf grabbed her wrists, grinning down at her as she struggled to pull away. Her hair fell into her laughing face. "Almost two hours."

Chapter 9

SEVEN WATCHED THE *Negh'Var* leave orbit from her narrow cabana on board the *Siren's Song*. Finally she would have some privacy after sharing a bed with Marani on the *Negh'Var.* The Bajoran crew seemed pleased to be back in command of their own vessel. The enthusiasm level ran high in the corridors, though Kira complained that everything seemed cramped after being on the *Negh'Var* for so long.

Seven believed she was the only person on board who was concerned about possible retaliation from those whom Kira had angered during the tour. The *Siren's Song* had heavy armament and fast legs, but the cruiser was weak compared to the great Alliance starships tethered in the orbiting Utopia Planitia shipyards. Kira had tried to requisition a battleship to accompany her back to Bajor, but Worf had refused. As Regent, he controlled the fleet, and he was not willing to give any military power to Kira.

Seven's own sense of survival could not be silenced. In the past she had endured more dangerous situations in order to complete her mission. Yet traveling on the *Siren's Song* disturbed her on a deep and persistent level.

As the *Negh'Var* disappeared beyond the orange arc of Jupiter, her anxiety increased in spite of her attempts to curb it.

"Seven!" Kira called from the adjoining chamber. "Come here."

Seven went through the ornate pool chamber, a miniature replica of the one on board Terok Nor, and entered the long common room. Kira was at the computer terminal.

"Do you know this man?" Kira demanded, pointing to a still image on the screen. The heavy brow ridge and slicked dark hair instantly reduced Seven to trembling like a seven-year-old.

"That's Ghemor, my foster father," Seven replied. He looked much older. The harsh lines around his mouth were grooved deep and the ridges on his chin were cragged with age. She could almost hear his booming voice ordering her to stand still. She had lived with his family for less than a standard year before being sent to the Obsidian Order training facility.

Kira was watching her, apparently enjoying her reaction. "He thinks I'm mistreating you."

Seven was glad Tain had prepared her for this or she would have been unable to restrain an incredulous retort. Ghemor had never liked her. He had sent her away the first chance he could wrest her from his grieving wife. "Ghemor contacted you? Why?"

"That's what I'd like to know," Kira told her. "Have you been sending messages to Cardassia?"

Seven clasped her hands behind her. "I have not contacted my foster family for many years. They made it clear they don't want me in Cardassian territory."

Kira leaned back in her chair, swiveling toward her. "I've done nothing but help you. I rescued you from that dingy moon, I fixed your ship and gave you a place to stay. I even brought you on this magnificent tour . . . yet you complain."

"I have not complained," Seven said evenly. "I'm grateful for everything you've done for me."

Kira gestured to the screen. "Then what's this?"

Seven frowned slightly as she looked at Ghemor. "Perhaps my foster family received reports from the Cardassian entourage at the Alliance Celebration. Or from Gul Dukat. Those are the only Cardassians I've seen."

Kira shifted uneasily, likely remembering how she had dressed Seven as a Cardassian Gul to provoke Dukat. "Pride . . . maybe that explains it. This Ghemor was practically rude, claiming I keep you locked up unless you're running around naked. What does he want? You live a life of luxury."

Seven shrugged. It was impossible to explain. Kira's prejudice against Terrans was so ingrained that she couldn't see Seven as anything but a slave.

"I've a good mind to tell him to jump into a wormhole," Kira grumbled.

Seven raised one brow. "Ghemor controls a significant faction on the Detapa Council, one that has opposed Gul Dukat. He could be a valuable ally."

"True. You are so smart, Seven. We should play nice and see what happens." Kira took her hand and patted it. "Why don't you send a message to Ghemor and tell him you're happy with the way I'm treating you?"

Seven knew that had been an order. "If you wish."

Kira kept looking at her. "You are happy, aren't you?"

"Yes . . ."

Kira seized on her note of hesitancy, as Seven knew she would. "Yes, but . . . what?"

Seven knew this was her chance. "Perhaps someone observed that I am not comfortable in this clothing." She gestured to the sheer, loose layers of fabric that currently exposed her legs and arms.

Kira examined her from head to toe. "You do look a little absurd, standing there at attention in your linens."

"I also don't like wearing a uniform I am not entitled to wear. I would be more comfortable in my pilot's jumper."

Kira thought about it for a moment then gestured a fond dismissal.

"I'll have Marani whip up a special outfit for you. I didn't like you as a Gul anyway . . . maybe there's something better." Kira waved her away. "And don't bother sending a message to your foster father. I'll handle it."

Seven knew Kira was being perverse by dressing her in traditional Cardassian body armor. Yet there was an immediate change in the way she was treated when she appeared wearing armor rather than the frivolous slave outfits Kira had lately preferred. Even the commander of the *Siren's Song* nodded respectfully when they met. Seven took comfort in the thin titanium plating on her body reminding her that she was no longer vulnerable.

Yet it also brought back memories of the years she had trained in the Obsidian Order, when she was trying to get used to the unfamiliar ridges on her face. Since she was a young child she had worn armor and obeyed Enabran Tain. Often it had been a struggle between life and death to become Cardassian, to acquire the Cardassian photographic memory, and surrender all personal desires. Those memories lay dormant yet vivid, waiting only for the association of the armor to bring them to the fore.

Kira also began treating her differently. She invited Seven to the farewell dinners hosted by various Alliance officials in Sol. Now Seven was introduced as a companion rather than ignored as a slave. Kira never acknowledged that she had changed her behavior toward Seven. But several times she mentioned Seven's association with Ghemor and his position on the Detapa Council. Seven believed Kira was in touch with her foster father.

Tain had involved Ghemor to protect her, but Seven didn't like it. She didn't want anything from him.

However, it worked. Seven was right where she needed to be, a guest at the table the night Kira dropped a torpedo on the farewell gathering. "Deanna is coming with me on the next leg of our tour," Kira enthused. "We're going to Alpha Centauri, Tellar, Tau Ceti, and Betazed . . ."

Seven thought she was foolish to outline their itinerary, but Kira was apparently not concerned. B'Elanna almost choked on her *gagh*, while Troi merely smiled and looked down at her plate.

B'Elanna pointedly ignored Kira and the others seated at the long table. Her voice was almost too low for Seven to hear as she asked Troi, "I thought I was taking you to Betazed."

"It's on my way," Kira said for Troi. "It will only take a few extra days to make a stop here and there."

"I'll be traveling on the *Sitio*," Troi calmly clarified.

"So I guess we're going together." Kira laughed in B'Elanna's face. "The more the merrier, I always say. Anyone else want to come?"

Amid the hurried, polite refusals from the other guests, B'Elanna flushed so darkly she looked like a full-blooded Klingon. Seven was impressed by Kira's tactical ability. It would be highly advantageous to have the flagship of Sol escorting them through the most populous corridor of the Alpha Quadrant. Perhaps Kira was not so oblivious to the danger as she seemed.

But Seven could not understand why Deanna Troi had agreed to accompany her. B'Elanna apparently didn't understand either. The Klingon was the first to leave the party that night, but Seven noted that Kira and Troi were always in proximity to one another. They rarely spoke, but when they did, there seemed to be an accord between them that Seven had not previously observed. They smiled at one another, exchanging glances over a comment someone else made.

This was a new development. It differed from the analysis that Seven had recently given Tain. Then, she thought Kira might be prepared to kill Troi. Now she could see that her assumption was wrong.

By the time they returned to Kira's ship, Seven was deeply disturbed. She believed her judgment had become impaired by the stress of using her own life as a cover. Tonight when someone had causally mentioned Ghemor to her, she had nearly bitten her tongue. She was too accustomed to hiding her former life on Cardassian.

Nothing was right anymore.

The tenor of the grand tour changed after they stopped traveling on the *Negh'Var*. Instead, the two midsized vessels joined the heavy traffic through the central corridor between Sol and Tau Ceti. Kira entertained various dignitaries on board the *Siren's Song,* and occasionally beamed down to a planet. Seven was accustomed to these rummage tours by now, and would silently take anything Kira gave her whether their hosts consented or not. Eventually, they would consent.

When they arrived on Tau Ceti Four, eight light-years away from Sol, Deanna Troi joined them for Kira's usual cultural tour. B'Elanna hastily included herself, arriving at the beam-down point with six Klingon guards.

As the tour progressed, Seven realized that the Klingon guards were in protective positions around B'Elanna and Troi, leaving Kira exposed. As a trained assassin, she could see the holes in the coverage that would allow a weapon to fix on Kira.

Seven stayed near B'Elanna and Troi. Kira didn't seem to notice. Her other slaves and those two Vulcan eunuchs always surrounded her, giving her the illusion of protection.

Then the Tau Ceti Intendant brought them to a large plaza and offered hoverpads so they could see the extensive rings of botanical gardens that intersected the capital city. B'Elanna refused. "I've had enough sightseeing for today."

But Kira was holding a whispered conference with Troi, and she turned to say, "That's fine. You can wait here while Deanna and I see the gardens."

"I'm tired of recycled air," Troi agreed, stepping onto her hoverpad.

"Would you like me to come with you?" Seven asked Kira, looking for a hoverpad she could use.

Kira stepped onto hers. "No, stay here." She winked in B'Elanna's direction. "You two have plenty in common."

Before Seven knew what was happening, Kira and Troi had zipped off together on their hoverpads, leaving everyone else behind. They disappeared among the wooded, winding paths. On the large plaza, the guards and slaves milled aimlessly, at a loss for what to do.

"It better be safe," B'Elanna grimly told the Tau Ceti Intendant. The older woman nervously assured B'Elanna that no one else had been allowed in the gardens for several days in preparation for their tour. B'Elanna didn't seem impressed by her claim that her people had run security sweeps before their arrival.

Seven wandered around the edge of the plaza, admiring the large iridescent black blooms, and the unusual plant formations. The shade was dappled and a refreshing breeze was stirring the leaves.

She waited until B'Elanna was also alone, standing with her arms crossed by the beam-out point, before moving closer. "I wish we could return to the ship," Seven said, knowing that was what B'Elanna wanted.

B'Elanna grunted. "This isn't safe."

"Kira is careless," Seven agreed.

"That doesn't mean she should endanger Deanna!" B'Elanna retorted.

"She is trying to annoy you."

"Me? She should worry about Worf, not me. She'll get Deanna killed with this childish behavior." B'Elanna's eyes narrowed.

"I do not understand why Deanna Troi chooses to be with Kira," Seven said, again voicing B'Elanna's thoughts. The Klingon was easy to read. There was no dissemblance in her nature.

"When you figure it out, let me know." B'Elanna shook her head in frustration. "You're a Free-Terran, why do you stay with her?"

Seven grimaced. "Free-Terrans don't have many choices." She lowered her eyes, knowing she was taking a big risk. But Tain had ordered her to make closer contact with Alliance officials. "I admire the way you have risen above your Terran heritage. Sometimes I hate myself for my blood. I feel Cardassian, and yet I betray myself with this face."

Seven didn't realize it was true until she said it.

"I'm Klingon," B'Elanna insisted. She almost reacted in anger, as at Spock's shrine when Kira had taunted her. But B'Elanna merely added, "Sometimes I have to fight to prove it."

"And now you're the Intendant of Sol, the most prized possession of the former Terran Empire. It shows what loyalty means to Klingons."

"I honor the houses of Duras and Worf," B'Elanna agreed. "They in turn have honored me."

"You have a post that you earned. Kira sits uneasy as Overseer because she takes things she doesn't deserve."

"Dangerous talk for someone so close to Kira," B'Elanna pointed out.

Seven scuffed one titanium-toed boot against the brick paving. "I thought I could speak honestly with you. Forgive me if I was mistaken."

She quickly withdrew, knowing that would tantalize B'Elanna. Better to leave her questioning, wanting to talk to her more. After all, they would have plenty of time together during the continuing tour.

Chapter 10

KIRA WOKE TO feel fingers running through her hair. For a moment she was at peace, sustained only by the tender stroking and the faint sound of wind rushing through the reeds. She had never felt so relaxed . . . lying with her head pillowed in Deanna Troi's lap.

"Umm . . ." Kira's eyes were closed, not wanting to return. "I remember someone doing this when I was young."

Deanna's hand slipped around Kira's waist, holding her close as she continued to stroke her hair. She whispered, "Was it your mother?"

Kira's eyes opened, and slowly she stretched and yawned. They were on the Betazed home planet, in the water gardens of the Fifth House, where Deanna had grown up. Occupied with sitting up and re-settling her foil headband, Kira didn't look at Deanna. She wanted to ignore the question, but she knew Deanna would feel her wariness. Offhandedly, she replied, "I didn't have a mother."

"No mother?" Deanna laughed lightly. "Wait until later, when you meet mine. I'd say you were lucky."

Kira hesitated before getting up, already regretting her lie. She lifted Deanna's hand, loving the way her heart was opening to Deanna.

"Thank you." Kira kissed her hand, then abruptly got up and strode to the beam-out point. She had delayed her departure too many times already. Kira looked back at Deanna for a few long seconds, waiting for the transporter to lock. Then she dematerialized.

Back on board the *Siren's Song*, Kira performed her duties. She gave orders to the commander to maintain orbit around Betazed, checked on Seven's latest supply and demand numbers, and told the slaves what to prepare for her evening meal. But despite the boring routine, she felt an unaccustomed joy. Especially when she considered the fact that she had just fallen asleep with the woman who had conspired to have her killed.

Yet a smile curved her lips every time she thought of Deanna. Her instincts couldn't be wrong. She believed that Winn's accomplices had cleverly led her astray by implicating Deanna Troi. Now she wondered who had really been behind that assassination plot. The accusation against Troi had been carefully designed to keep her suspicious of the one person in the galaxy who could understand and help her. Deanna was a wealth of information about the Intendants and Alliance officials.

Kira's path had been smoothed ever since the Alliance Celebration, when Deanna had performed some miracle, allowing her to keep the Vulcan twins.

As Kira leaned over Seven's shoulder, her eyes glazed at the mind-boggling rows of numbers that indicated the flow of latinum, dilithium, and other precious commodities in the Alliance. She was really thinking about Deanna. The way those dark eyes could draw her in . . . how her glossy black ringlets fell against her smooth cheek. And her hands, so strong and capable, yet so small that Kira sometimes felt as if she were holding the hand of a vulnerable child.

Their relationship had taken an extraordinary turn while they were still in the Alpha Centauri system. Deanna had appropriated the planetarium, one of the most complex holosimulators anywhere, for their own private use. The antigrav units made it feel as if they were flying through space without the aid of a starship. There was only the two of them and the galactic phenomenon passing by: orange and blue suns, starburst novas, and planets being bombarded by meteorites.

The simulation surpassed every expectation. Together they had glided through the wonders of the universe. Kira felt weightless and free, and they had laughed the entire time.

Then Deanna told her to close her eyes and drift. Kira did as she asked, wondering what would happen.

Kira had never felt anything like it. She was floating in the air, no pressure on her feet or pull against her body. All she could do was float.

Then Deanna curled around her, her arms enveloping her, and Kira knew she had found her equal. She knew she was finally complete.

Kira realized she wasn't paying any attention when Seven turned to her. "You're not interested in this data."

"No, I'm not," Kira happily admitted. She impulsively slipped her arms around Seven, but the Terran was not as enchanting as she used to be. After all, she was only Terran, not even comparable to Deanna Troi.

Kira gave Seven a final pat. At least the Terran was good at dealing with trade matters. The Overseer's duties seemed to grow increasingly complex rather than settling into a manageable flow. "It's almost time for our tour of Betazed. Would you like to come?"

Seven nodded seriously. "Few people have ever seen Betazed. I'm curious about their culture."

"Well, we've got Deanna to explain everything." Kira didn't mention that she particularly wanted to meet Deanna's mother.

Lwaxana Troi was not what Kira expected. Where Deanna was bold and confident, her mother was cowed and fearful. Deanna was a head shorter than Lwaxana, yet she carried herself like royalty. Lwaxana tended to jump at the slightest sound as if she wanted to run. Actually, Deanna's mother looked Terran, except for her very dark eyes, with curling reddish hair and smooth features. Kira saw her attraction to Deanna in a new light. She had always been titillated by the baby-faced species, and Deanna had both their innocent appearance and a will to match her own.

Kira wasn't sure if Lwaxana was more typical of Betazoids than Deanna because they met no other people during the tour. As the group strolled through the vacant arcades and echoing ceremonial halls, they saw no signs of life. As they flew light-flyers over vast residential complexes, surrounded by agricultural greenhouses, Kira quietly asked Seven about the population. Seven estimated that at least five hundred million people lived on the planet, but only Lwaxana and Deanna revealed themselves. At first it was strange viewing an abandoned planet, but it quickly grew tiresome.

"I want to meet more Betazoids," Kira demanded. "I don't care about architectural façades."

Deanna nodded regretfully. "Our people are sensitive to strangers. This isn't a criticism of you but of us. They flee from the unbridled thoughts and emotions that surround this group." Deanna gestured into the air as if their feelings were colored clouds that lowered over them. "We survive by training our children to buffer their thoughts and emotions. When we are very young, we begin learning how to build blocks to prevent being overwhelmed by others. With outworlders, it is more difficult."

"Why doesn't it bother you?" Kira asked.

"Deanna has always been strong," her mother murmured. Then she looked frightened, as if she shouldn't have said anything.

Deanna smiled at Lwaxana, but without much

warmth. "Most Betazoids would rather die than leave this planet."

B'Elanna had been silent throughout the tour, but this seemed to interest her. "You mean it hurts you to be around other people?"

"Yes," Deanna agreed. "It's ironic, really. Most people are afraid of empaths and telepaths, but we are the ones who must run away."

Kira insisted on meeting a planetary official, so a slender man was finally summoned to their light-flyer. He was cringing and blinking rapidly as he answered their questions. Kira found him so amusing she was almost tempted to annex him into her household. But knowing Deanna had given her a respect for Betazoids that made the impulse merely a private joke.

When the official gratefully bid them good-bye, she was convinced that Betazoids were no threat to the Alliance, despite what some alarmist paranoids tried to claim. Deanna had confided her own trouble with K'mpec, the former Klingon High Chancellor. He had accused Deanna of picking over his mind, when usually she was trying to block out his self-focused rage and hatred.

As Deanna thanked the Betazoid official, obviously keeping him from fleeing with unseemly haste, Kira found herself alone with Lwaxana. Kira was amused by her sudden trembling, rustling her long brocade skirts. Her fingertips nervously squeezed the round stones of her long necklace.

"Do you get to see Deanna often?" Kira asked her.

"No . . ." Lwaxana glanced at her daughter, who was

still occupied with the Betazoid official. "But lately she's been spending time on Betazed II, where New Hope is being built."

"Oh?" Kira had heard Troi mention New Hope in passing. "What's it like?"

"I've never been there." Lwaxana again glanced at Deanna. "But it's important to Deanna, so I helped her get the approval from the other Houses."

"I bet that wasn't easy," Kira said thoughtfully.

"Yes, we are reclusive, as you can see. The thought of a galactic resort on our fourth planet was somewhat daunting."

"I would think so." Kira turned to greet Deanna who was returning. "I'd like to see New Hope."

Deanna seemed taken aback for a moment, then she linked her arm through Kira's. "I was going to surprise you, but I might as well tell you now. I was going to order our ships to proceed to Betazed II so when you woke up tomorrow, we could breakfast on my favorite planet."

They were moving away from the rest of the entourage. B'Elanna's scowl was the only dark spot among the group. Seven was avidly feeding notes into her padd while Marani tried to keep the yawning slaves in line.

Kira murmured, "Let's go back to the *Siren's Song*. I have a yearning for some privacy. . . ."

New Hope was a delightful place with lavender skies and sheer cliffs rising from the emerald-green sea. It reminded Kira of their tour of Betazed, with beautiful yet empty concourses and entertainment centers. But around every corner were workers and Terran slaves, performing tasks from programming holo-murals to polishing brass grates.

The resort was constructed with luxurious materials that were responsive to the senses. The air temperature and ambient sound were carefully controlled. Even the flowers draped over the low bordering walls were cunningly chosen for their color and fragrance. As Kira walked through the resort, she passed through one delicious bouquet to the next.

Just as Deanna promised, Kira breakfasted with her on the terrace of her private home at one end of the resort. It had been an unforgettable night as they slowly cruised to Betazed II. Now they looked out on Winamay Falls and the great crescent curve of the hanging gardens that cascaded down a thousand meters to the sea. A pleasant hum rose from something called *lappas,* mingling with the rush of water from the falls.

Kira longed to tell Deanna that she had been implicated in the assassination attempt by Winn's accomplices. She even wanted to talk to Deanna about her own mother, Meru. For once in her life, Kira wanted to have no secrets, no suspicions. But she had never been that honest with anyone, and she didn't know how to start.

"Your resort will be a wonderful success." Kira waved toward the sea-cliff view. "I think people will come from across the galaxy to enjoy this."

Deanna, murmured, "Umm . . . I hope so."

"When did you get the idea for a resort?" Kira asked.

"Oh, a long time ago. When I first visited this planet,

I thought it was a waste that only I could see it." A small frown line appearing between her eyes. "But I spent a fortune building it."

"I couldn't imagine anything less." Kira gestured to the white arches of the buildings hugging the top of the cliffs. The open plazas were strategically situated for maximum vistas. Everything was done in the best of taste.

"It should work out fine, except . . ."

"Except what?" Kira asked curiously. She had never seen Deanna so hesitant before.

"I need the gaming license for this sector in order to make New Hope viable. Otherwise I won't get the top rating and the best people won't come."

Kira sat back in her seat. "Who holds the license?"

"You do," Deanna told her.

Kira almost denied it; then she remembered one of the first things she had done as Overseer. She had canceled the independent "agent fees" and routed all gaming licenses through her office. That had released a lot of licenses and her staff had snapped up as many as they could.

"I do?" Kira asked slowly.

"You can understand how important it is to have gaming as an integral part of the resort."

"I see." Kira felt her mouth go dry, and she didn't like it. It was hard to speak. "I mean, I can see how important it is to you."

Kira waited, almost expecting Deanna to point out that she hadn't asked her for anything. Deanna had always given. Given her time, her affection, her experience, her advice . . . it was a relatively minor thing to ask for in exchange.

Yet Kira felt a chill in the air that she hadn't noticed before. The sky seemed less vivid and the scents more cloying.

Kira stood up. She couldn't sit next to Deanna when the empath must be sensing her turbulent reaction. She calmed herself, smiling down. "I'll go right now and look into this."

Deanna nodded, but the magic sympatico between them had disappeared. As if it had never really existed. "I look forward to your return."

Kira transported up to the *Siren's Song,* leaving Deanna on Betazed II. As she materialized, Bajoran curses exploded from her. Inside she was crying—betrayed!

She shoved past everyone, and they scattered before her with fear in their eyes. In the tiny office off the common room, Seven was standing at the computer terminal, as usual.

"When were you hired by Winn Adami?" Kira demanded.

Seven raised one brow. "I would have to consult my ship's log for the exact stardate."

"Do it," Kira ordered. "And find out the stardate when I voided the agent fees and took over the gaming licenses."

Kira threw herself on the sofa in the common room, waiting for Seven to reappear. She couldn't think. She didn't want to believe it was true. Then Seven silently handed her a padd with the information. Seven had been contacted by Jadzia on behalf of Leeta and Ziyal only three days after Kira had assumed control of the gaming licenses.

Checking further, Kira saw that the agent for the gaming licenses for Betazed and the surrounding sectors used to be Deanna Troi. She had signed a hefty contract with the Ferengi Grand Nagus during the Alliance gathering, shortly before Kira had been made Overseer. Large latinum commitments had already been made regarding the construction of New Hope on Betazed II.

Kira's lips went white. "Get out!" she shouted at Seven, leaping to her feet as if to strike her. The other slaves quickly slipped away as Kira screamed in frustration.

She had been manipulated. Lwaxana was right—the most important thing to Deanna Troi was New Hope. Kira had been holding the key without knowing it. Troi must have wanted her killed to get her precious gaming license. When that didn't work, she had tried seduction to get what she wanted. And Kira had fallen for it like some back-space rube. Betrayed . . .

Chapter 11

AFTER KIRA ORDERED everyone to leave, Seven gathered her padd and a special data disk and went directly to the transporter room of the *Siren's Song*. She requested permission to beam aboard B'Elanna's ship.

Kira's terrible reaction indicated that the situation could change. Seven had seen Troi's name among the former agents who held gaming licenses. Because of link in the stardates, Kira must have assumed the licenses had something to do with the assassination attempt.

Seven considered Kira's behavior to be irrational; first accepting Seven into her inner circle then seeking a relationship with Deanna Troi, when both had been involved in Winn's assassination plot. It made no sense, yet her Obsidian Order training had taught Seven that people often pursued the very thing that would bring about their destruction.

It took only a matter of moments for Seven to receive permission to transport. It was a testament to her growing friendship with B'Elanna. She had been spending most of her free time on board the *Sitio*. Often she engaged in hand-to-hand combat simulations with B'Elanna, or they talked, usually about Worf and things that were happening in the Klingon territory. B'Elanna got regular reports about the ritual ceremonies as Gowron was formally made High Chancellor. She sometimes seemed wistful about not being on Qo'noS.

Their friendship had first warmed, ironically enough, when Seven made an off-color remark about Kira's growing fascination with Deanna Troi. It was while they were still orbiting Alpha Centauri Six, when Troi and Kira went to the magnificent planetarium together to experience the complex holo-environment. When B'Elanna said that Worf would soon leave Klingon territory, Seven had muttered something about a ménage à Troi.

B'Elanna had sputtered with laughter. "It wouldn't be the first time! Worf may love women, but he only trusts Deanna Troi. Kira won't be around for long. I've seen it before."

Seven admired B'Elanna's ability to be a loyal friend to both Worf and Troi in spite of her absolute hatred of Kira. B'Elanna seemed to appreciate Seven's grasp of the situation.

Now, as Seven materialized on board B'Elanna's flagship, she felt as if she were unfurling from a cramped and uncomfortable confinement. She could finally drop the subservient, admiring attitude that Kira demanded of her. No one on board the *Sitio* ever ordered her to smile or to relax, as Kira did.

In B'Elanna's company, Seven felt as if she was finally discovering her own true nature. At least she was expressing her own impulses and desires. The cloying confusion that had stifled every thought was brushed aside by something clear and honest. She could be brusque with B'Elanna, who was never offended by her short answers or precise assessments. They sometimes argued over issues of production, supply and demand, which occupied much of B'Elanna's time as well Seven's. Yet they could also sit for an hour on end in companionable silence.

Seven knew that Enabran Tain would say she was weakened by her sincere regard for B'Elanna. But she trusted the Klingon-Terran, and paradoxically that made her feel stronger. It was as if she had never acted on her own before, and she was stumbling straight into adulthood from being a small child.

B'Elanna was behaving like a true friend. They had even discussed their mutual self-hatred of their Terran heritage. It had been late one night after they fought each other sweaty and nearly blind with fatigue during a high-level simulation. Their self-loathing drove them against one another. It finally began to ease when Seven found herself against such a resolute, immovable force. B'Elanna seemed to feel similarly satisfied after that night.

B'Elanna's newest aide stepped aside, allowing Seven into her quarters without announcing her. B'Elanna was reclining on a lounge with a cup of Klingon *pipius* tea in one hand and her padd in the other. It was a familiar sight.

"Here, this is for you." Seven held out the data disk. "It is an efficiency report I have created for the Sol system. With this information, you can make changes that would increase productivity by nearly fourteen percent."

"What?" B'Elanna stared at her incredulously.

Seven continued to hold out the disk. "It is an efficiency report for the Sol System."

B'Elanna took the disk. "I heard you, I just couldn't believe it." She popped it into her padd and scanned the data. Her eyes grew intent. "You've done a lot of work here."

"It is incomplete; however, *now* seemed like a good time to give it to you." Seven took a seat across from B'Elanna. She wished she could simply ask B'Elanna for asylum on the *Sitio*. B'Elanna would agree, but Kira would never let her go so easily. Seven knew too much about too many things. She would have to find a clean escape.

B'Elanna was shaking her head over the data, obviously pleased with the thorough analysis. "You'd make a better Overseer than Kira," she wryly commented.

"I am already performing the duties that the Overseer is required to do."

"Really?" B'Elanna raised one brow, distracted for a moment from the padd. "You do know more about galactic trade than anyone I know."

"Kira is incapable of reading a simple profit-and-loss statement," Seven said severely. "Surely you haven't believed that Kira was doing any work? She exists merely to gather objets d'art and new slaves."

That was a sure hit. B'Elanna glowered at the thought of the Vulcan twins, now out of her reach. "I should have known! So that reorganization of the Benzar-Loren corridor was your idea?"

"Yes, and the K'taran trade agreement. And the relocation of the rendering plant to the mining site on Kalla II. And the reorganized trade route between the colony worlds."

"And nobody knows it was you." B'Elanna shook her head.

"Kira claims responsibility," Seven said flatly. "Yet she grows jealous of my knowledge of the Alliance territory."

"Very interesting," B'Elanna mused. "I wish Worf was here . . . I got a message from him yesterday. He's at top warp and should meet up with us in a couple of weeks."

They sat in silence, both staring into the passing starfield with the arc of Betazed II curving below them. The door hissed and B'Elanna's aide entered. The aide hesitated, then blurted out, "What's wrong?"

B'Elanna glanced at Seven, her lip curving up on one side. "When something's wrong, we'll tell you," B'Elanna retorted, laughing at her aide. "Bring us bloodwine!"

As the aide hurried to fetch the flagons, B'Elanna told Seven, "I have an urge to celebrate with you."

Seven remembered a quote inscribed in the *Sitio*'s conference room. " 'Let's share a draft together for the galaxy is large and the future unknown.' "

They both smiled, and Seven knew that whatever else happened, she had found a friend in B'Elanna. She had helped Seven express herself and become a better person. For that, Seven would always be grateful.

* *˘ *

Seven was summoned back to Kira's ship not long afterward, but she had given B'Elanna the gift. She had also shared a drink with her friend.

So Seven didn't blink when she entered the quarters on the *Siren's Song* and saw Kira tearing the very fabric from the walls. Kira was in a fury, smashing objects and slashing cushions with her knife.

The slaves huddled on the far side of the room, shifting as Kira moved, obviously afraid they would be the next possessions rendered into bits. The Vulcan twins were expressionless, all skinny legs and big staring eyes, standing side by side with their shoulders barely touching. The youngest Terran boy was crying. Marani stayed between the others and Kira, coming forward sometimes as if wanting to somehow soothe her mistress.

When Kira saw Seven, she seemed to snap out of it. Ignoring the evidence of her loss of control, she ordered, "Go to the bridge and tell the commander that we've been summoned to meet the Regent. Have her plot a course toward Klingon territory."

Seven nodded, her hands clasped behind her. She wouldn't question why Kira wanted her to personally inform the captain rather than calling through the comm. "Shall I also notify the *Sitio* of our departure?"

"No." Kira had a speculative expression, detached from everything around her. "I'll do that."

Kira turned and retreated to the tiny office where Seven had been performing the Overseer's duties since leaving the *Negh'Var*. Seven wondered if Kira would restrain herself or attack that room as well. She was not concerned; the data she had gathered was stored in her implant database. It was priceless information. Often she thought of how pleased Enabran Tain would be when her database was downloaded.

Seven performed her task, and the bridge crew leaped into action. The commander ordered a course set for Klingon territory until Kira could provide more specific coordinates. For security reasons, the Regent rarely informed anyone of his whereabouts or projected flight path. Seven was on the bridge when the ship left orbit and engaged full impulse out of the Betazed system.

When Seven reported back, Kira wasn't in her quarters. The slaves were carefully removing the signs of destruction. Seven knew Kira had probably retreated to the small arboretum on deck seven, but she decided to remain and help the slaves clean up.

She consciously defied her training, knowing that people were unguarded when they were enraged. Kira could be prodded into revealing vital information, such as where the portal was located. But Seven couldn't seek out confidences from Kira. Every personal inclination resisted the idea.

At that moment, Seven began to consider options for terminating her mission. She had gotten a great deal of information so Tain wouldn't consider it a failure. But she had never voluntarily sought the end of an undercover assignment. She knew it was disobedient, that she was betraying her oath to the Obsidian Order, but her well-honed mind could not stop searching of its own accord for a way out.

* * *

It took several days before Seven could access the messages Kira had sent prior to leaving Betazed II. First, there was the damage to the quarters to repair; then Kira demanded everyone's absolute attention. She wanted constant entertainment, yet nothing held her interest. She even stopped a passing slave ship and acquired two new Terrans and a beautiful young Vulcan woman. Kira engaged in a frenzy of pleasure, though Seven was dubious as to whether she truly enjoyed it.

Seven was relieved when Kira suggested that she should tend to the Overseer's duties. With the door to the small office closed, Seven was finally at peace with her columns of numbers, names, and coordinates.

With hardly any effort, her implant decrypted Kira's security block on the messages. Kira had sent the first to B'Elanna. It was fairly short and straightforward. Kira claimed she had to go to the Zakdorn system, where she and Worf were going to consult with the greatest strategic minds in the galaxy about the complex economic system run by the Alliance. Kira added that she would be returning to Bajor after that.

Since B'Elanna had been eager to get away from Kira, she would resist any urging from Deanna to follow her. Seven was disappointed that she would not see B'Elanna again. She did approve of consulting with the Zakdorns about certain Overseer problems she had encountered. Yet something was not right.

Seven activated Kira's next message. It was for Deanna Troi. Kira said basically the same thing. Her tone was flippant yet distracted, as if a load of work had suddenly descended on her. But Kira leaned closer at the end of the message and added in a breathy voice, "I'm upset that I can't spend more time with you in New Hope. But good news! I've checked into the Betazed gaming license, and it will only take a few days for it to be transferred to you. I simply must run back to Bajor, but maybe you can convince Worf to bring you to Terok Nor. I'll work on him while we're in Zakdorn." It was followed by a false display of affection before Kira signed off.

Sure enough, among the pile of work disks on the desk was an order from Kira to transfer the Betazed sector gaming license to Deanna Troi. Once a record was made of the transaction, there would be a three-standard-day waiting period for public posting; then the license would belong to Troi. Seven completed the procedure and posted the official announcement.

Later that evening, Kira sauntered into the office. "Did you take care of the Betazed gaming license?"

"Yes." Seven was standing at the computer terminal, as usual. "The announcement has been posted."

"It's not likely that anyone will contest my ownership of the license," Kira commented. "How long before it's official?"

Seven pretended to consult the chrono, though her implant instantly gave her the answer. "Two days, eighteen hours, and twenty-three minutes."

"You sent a note to Deanna?"

"It is part of the official requirements," Seven patiently pointed out.

"Good." Kira smiled to herself. "We had a nice little vacation, didn't we? How long will it take you to catch up on everything here?"

Seven raised one brow. "At least another day and a half."

"Good. When you're finished, let me know. I have another job I think you can do for me."

Seven dreaded the thought of Kira's job even as she methodically completed each task of the Overseer's duties. There was one bit of unexpected news from Garak on Terok Nor. Leeta had escaped from the mining facility. Seven knew that Kira was going to be livid when she found out, but she was glad that Leeta had managed to get away. Her reaction was irrational because Leeta should have meant nothing to her. Yet Seven was glad that someone close to First Minister Winn had survived her mission. Despite the fact that Leeta had contracted Seven to kill Kira, she seemed like an honorable person. Her motives for supporting Winn against Kira appeared to be altruistic, which was rare enough in this universe. So Seven actually smiled as she tagged the information for Kira to see.

When order had finally been restored, Seven reported to the common room.

Kira languidly rose from the sofa and gestured her toward the inner sanctum. Slaves were lying about the common room, mostly sleeping. One of the boy slaves whimpered in his sleep, while the new Terran was curled into a tense ball, watching every move Kira made. Marani was keeping an eye on him.

Seven followed Kira into the inner sanctum. Kira sealed the door behind them. "You're finished?"

"Operations are running smoothly." Seven steeled herself.

"Good." Kira went to the wall and let the laser light flash against her cornea. The door to the panel vault swung open, and Kira pulled out a dark blue case.

Seven instantly recognized it. The portal.

"I want you to kill B'Elanna," Kira ordered.

Seven had prepared herself for something like this. But it was still a surprise. "B'Elanna? I don't understand. The *Sitio* is in the Betazed system, isn't it?"

"Yes, but this portal is Iconian. It can teleport you instantly across light-years. I forgot you only went down to Bajor to take care of Winn. When I first got it, I sent a slave all the way to Romulus." Kira opened up the clamshell device, letting Seven see the mirror. "You could be there in seconds."

Seven hesitated. "Are you sure it's safe?"

"Yes, now hurry," Kira insisted.

"How do you want me to do it?" Seven asked.

"I don't care, as long as it's done." Kira seemed impatient as she held up the portal. "We don't have much time."

Seven felt an eagerness she tried to conceal as she glanced into the mirror. All she had to do was think about B'Elanna and she would be safe. Tain wouldn't get the portal, but she didn't care. The important thing was getting off the *Siren's Song*.

She concentrated on her memories of B'Elanna, sitting in her quarters with her padd in one hand and *pipius* tea in the other. The mirrored surface started to cloud.

Abruptly Kira closed the portal.

"What's wrong?" Seven asked, feeling a sinking inside.

"Aren't you worried about how you'll get back?" Kira asked.

Seven felt caught. Of course she hadn't considered that.

Kira pressed a button on her desk and the door to the inner sanctum slid open. Two security guards were waiting with their phaser pistols drawn. "Put her in the 'fresher," Kira ordered. "Don't make any record of this arrest."

Seven wanted to try to escape, but the pistols blocked her only way out. They would stun her before she could grab the portal from Kira and teleport away.

Reluctantly, she started to the 'fresher. "I don't understand. I told you I will do anything for you."

Kira placed the portal on her desk and followed Seven toward the 'fresher. "I think you've lost your edge. I don't think you would kill anyone, let alone your new friend B'Elanna."

Seven drew in her breath. So that was it. "I've done everything you asked. I would never betray you."

"You can't do it," Kira said flatly. "You've lost your edge."

Seven pressed her lips together rather than blurt out the truth. Killing Winn had been wrong. It had haunted her sleep and disturbed her days as nothing else ever had. It felt as if another person had performed her previous missions using her body. But *she* had killed Winn. Kira knew the truth—Seven never wanted to harm anyone again.

Kira gestured her to go inside the 'fresher. Seven stepped into the small room, desperate. "I'd do anything for you, Kira. I always have. Why won't you believe me?"

"Because you don't want to come back." Kira sounded angry.

"You arranged everything last time," Seven protested. "I trust you. I would do anything to get back to you."

Kira's expression was sour. "I don't trust you, Seven. Getting back would be easy. If you hold onto the portal, it will go through with you."

Seven glanced at the portal, struck by the myriad of possibilities that offered. "Let me try—"

"To kill B'Elanna?" Kira asked. "You wouldn't. I know more than you think, Seven. I always have."

The door of the 'fresher slid closed in Seven's face. The locking mechanism made a faint click. She was left alone in the tiny room, with the mirrored walls and ceiling creating a series of distortions that Kira seemed to love.

Seven sat on the cushioned bench, staring at herself reflected over and over again. She was in the unaccountable position of being unable to do anything to help herself. She had betrayed her cover identity in her desire to get off the *Siren's Song*. She should have realized Kira was testing her and not been so eager. It was her own fault she was now trapped.

Chapter 12

TROI WAS HAPPIER than she ever thought possible. After so much effort, holding her tongue and pretending at love games, she had finally gotten the gaming license for her sector. Tomorrow it would officially belong to her to assign however she wished.

It was true that Kira's first reaction had not been good. But Troi had discovered that Kira's temper tantrums were quick to come and go.

The latest communiqué from Kira had arrived yesterday, and everything was fine. Troi figured a trip to Bajor would seal her hold on Kira. She intended to ask Worf to take her to that distant sector very soon.

As for now, with Kira gone, time was her own again. She checked every rivet and mechanical device installed in New Hope. As she lovingly examined the innovative medical center, running her hand along the biobeds and computer interface, she thought about the Chief Medical Officer she would hire. Dr. Aad was, among other things, an obstetrician with expertise in interspecies birth processes. The CEO of the resort had opened negotiations for a five-standard-year contract.

Troi hugged her arms around herself, smiling at the thought of spending more time in this beautiful room with the gentle pink-tinted light and comforting rows of computer sensors. She had always wanted to have a baby with Worf. New Hope would enable her to do it.

As she paused at the doorway, she knew that it wasn't the lack of medical equipment or qualified care that had stopped her. She could have asked Dr. Aad to work on Worf's flagship. And the medical facility would have been even easier to create. But it wasn't that simple.

She left the medical center, strolling down the slightly cushioned path between the rows of glistening *sippis* buds, bursting with a tangy scent. The arc of the security shield had finally been adjusted and it no longer interfered with the ever-changing hues of the sky. It had been too blue yesterday, and Troi had worked with the technicians for hours to get it right. She was pleased to see that tonight's sunset was undistorted.

A maximum-security shield extended over the complex and down into the water to the bedrock. This had the added benefit of stilling the violent waves at the base of the cliffs and cutting down on the moisture in the air. The wind force had also been damped so only a continuous tropical breeze carried salty fresh air across the resort. The raging winds of its pristine state had been dramatic, but not conducive to quiet moons-lit dinners or a snuggle in the rookeries.

Troi felt safe in New Hope. Her child wouldn't be exposed to battle or the strife of running the Alliance Armada. Her child would grow up in a stable, secure environment.

Cupping a *sippis* bloom in her hand, noting the delicate tracery of white veins amid the vivid blue, she knew she could face her greatest fear in this place. Worf might discover, through their child, that she was half-Terran. Would that change his love for her? Would he turn away from them both?

Her fear of rejection had kept her from attempting to have a child. The doctor would have to know her dual heritage in order to properly monitor and guide the development of the fetus. She could never have kept it from Worf on board the flagship, and she knew it was possible it would be revealed even when she completely controlled the environment. A secret told to one soon spreads to all.

But even if Worf rejected her, she would still have New Hope. It would become bittersweet, certainly, as her dreams of growing old with Worf were shattered and she mourned the one true love in her life. But she would have Worf's baby and would pour her love into him. New Hope would protect them. And she was certain that Worf would remember their love, and would be drawn to see their child. Surely Worf would forgive her for lying about her heritage. Here, on her beloved planet, Troi felt secure enough to face any challenge.

Keiko waved from the patio of her private home, on

the highest hill in New Hope. "A secured call has come for you, m'lady."

Troi straightened up. Worf made secured calls so no one could pinpoint his location. She brushed the blue dust of the *sippis* bloom from her hands and hurried home. Worf would be meeting Kira tomorrow in the Zakdorn system, and surely Kira would try to tease Worf about what had happened between her and Troi while he was on Qo'noS.

Troi decided to tell Worf now about her plans, to let him know in the most absolute terms that their future lay together. Whatever happened with Kira was unimportant. She knew he might become intimate with Kira, but as long as he was thinking about returning to her, to make a baby with her, it wouldn't matter.

Flushed and excited, she sat down at the computer. When Keiko withdrew, she activated the screen.

Gul Dukat appeared. *"Nice to see someone having a good time,"* he said bitterly. *"Most of us are not so fortunate."*

Troi immediately shifted into politician mode, not easy when she had been expecting something very different. "What can I do for you, Gul Dukat?"

"Now you don't look so happy." His gray skin looked chalky white, and the ridges were knobby as if the skin had tightened. *"That seems to be the story of my life. When I show up, the party stops."*

"I'm very busy right now—"

"Busy entertaining Kira Nerys?" Dukat asked. *"I heard you two have grown very close."*

"As a matter of fact, the Overseer left Betazed days ago. You can contact her on the *Siren's Song*."

"*So that's how it is now? You don't remember the conversation we had about Kira? You made it clear enough then what your feelings were.*"

Things had changed dramatically since then. Troi knew that she was better off with the Overseer resting in the palm of her hand. Ever wary that others would hear this exchange, including possibly Kira, Troi smoothly replied, "I have always been fascinated by Kira Nerys. My respect for her has only increased."

"*Stop this nonsense!*" Dukat exclaimed. "*We both know she has no experience or aptitude for the job of Overseer. She abuses her post.*"

Troi remembered telling B'Elanna almost exactly the same thing not long ago. "Those are serious accusations. I think you should discuss this with the Regent, not with me."

Dukat slammed his fist against the desk, shaking the monitor. But his tone was strangely hesitant.

"*Things are not going well for me on Cardassia Prime. Personal problems . . . I can't guarantee that I'll have the support I need to be appointed Overseer if we wait any longer.*" He seemed to realize he wasn't making an impact. "*We must move now against Kira. My last attempt failed; they couldn't get close to her. I need your help!*"

Troi spoke as if she were shocked. "What are you saying? I suggest you get some mental-health care immediately . . . or at least some sleep. You look like you're ready to collapse."

Dukat sat back, his body relaxing to the inevitable. *"You will not help me?"*

"I'm signing off now." Troi acted as if she was trying to be kind but was fast losing patience. "You need help, Gul Dukat. I'm worried about you."

Troi cut transmission, sitting back with a relieved "Whew! That was close . . ."

Suddenly from behind her, a familiar voice asked, "Yes, wasn't it? He could have really incriminated you, couldn't he?"

It was Kira! Troi leaped from her chair, turning to face Kira. It was really her.

"What are you doing here?" Deanna demanded, glancing from the closed door to the window. "How did you get in?"

"Questions, questions," Kira drawled. She was wearing some sort of pressurized suit and helmet, leaving only her face exposed. She settled an object resembling a round porthole securely on one hip. "No welcome-back kisses?"

Kira pulled an Andorian laser from her belt and pointed it at Troi.

Troi's mouth went dry. She couldn't sense anything for a moment through her own intense panic. She wanted to scream "HOW?!" How did Kira penetrate the best security the Alliance could offer?

Kira said flatly, "You conspired with Winn Adami to have me killed. When that didn't work, you conspired with Gul Dukat. Good thing his life fell apart on him, or it might have worked."

Troi's eyes widened, she couldn't help it. How did Kira know about Winn Adami?

Kira spit out, "I trusted you! You betrayed me from the start. It was all a lie, every word, every touch!"

"No!" Troi protested, her voice cracking. "It's not true. I'm in love with you."

Kira was completely self-possessed, cold and furious. Troi knew she was scrambling. Her very life depended on this moment. She had to convince Kira that she loved her.

She threw every feeling for Worf into her voice; her yearning for a baby and a life filled with love. She let it show in her eyes, her longing and her desire. Kira needed her love and depended on her strength.

"Kira, we've grown very close," Troi said softly, taking one step forward. Her hand raised as if she must touch her. "You've frightened me, but that doesn't change how I feel about you. I know we have something special."

Kira let her come each step closer, the laser lowering slightly as she looked at Troi's eyes and lips, lovingly searching every curve of her face.

"I love you," Troi murmured.

Kira raised the laser to Troi's chest, making her gasp. "No, you love this place, New Hope. You don't love anyone but yourself. And you've betrayed me for the last time."

Troi tried to protest, she tried to grab the laser, but the warmth hit her. A burning expanded through her chest and the world tilted out from under her.

She was falling away from Kira, unable to stop herself, hitting the floor with a bone-jarring thud. Her heart was beating faster, blood rushing through her ears. She thought desperately—*Worf! My Imzadi . . .*

Everything was blurry, until Kira's face swam closer. The Bajoran had tears running down her cheeks and her mouth moved, but Deanna couldn't hear what she said. Then it became her mother's face, wavering and looking concerned. Then all the people she had ever known or spoken to, and all the deeds she had done or shouldn't have done. Her dreams were disappearing one after the other like gossamer soap bubbles. The last was the laughing face of a half-Klingon baby.

With her final breath, she whispered, *"Imzadi . . ."*

Chapter 13

KIRA WIPED THE tears from her face with shaking hands. She mourned an illusion, something that was never real.

Without touching Deanna, she scanned the Betazoid to be sure she was dead. She looked very small lying there. For the first time, Kira wondered what Worf would do when he found out.

Sticking the laser and scanner to the belt of her vac-suit, Kira pulled out a dispenser that had been filled by the bio-sciences replicator on board the *Siren's Song*. It contained a mixture of dust and Andorian skin cells. Her vac-suit and hood would keep her own DNA from distributing around the room. Since she had visited New Hope not long ago, a certain amount of her DNA could be expected in Deanna's quarters, but tests were sensitive enough to pick out the most recent layers.

She quickly activated the injector, dispersing the incriminating Andorian DNA through the room, paying particular attention to the area near the door. Troi's servants would enter and leave, taking minute quantities of the evidence with them, spreading it throughout the resort. It would offer proof that one female and two male Andorians had infiltrated New Hope. It would appear they had exacted revenge against the Regent for humiliating the Andorians at the last Alliance gathering.

Looking at Deanna's crumpled body, ever mindful of the need to leave before her slaves returned, Kira still hesitated. She had never known anyone like Deanna before, and she wished it could have been real. Instead, the Betazoid had hypnotized her, controlled her like a puppet. She should have listened to the old folklore that warned of the dangers of telepaths. Kira intended to make sure none of them left their planet again to wreck havoc with innocent people's minds and emotions.

Holding the Iconian portal in front of her, she drew a deep breath and thought about Marani back on the *Siren's Song*. Marani's face swam into focus on the smooth mirrored surface. She was looking around in concern, exactly like the first time. Kira smiled as she felt the tug of the portal; then she started to fall toward Marani.

With a quick inversion, almost as if she had snapped inside out, Kira landed with a rush of air, hitting the deck of her quarters. The portal was still clutched in her hand. It supported her weight for a moment, until she could get her bearings.

She was dizzy and disoriented, but she waved Marani

away. "Help me off with this suit, then tell the commander to report to me immediately. I have something for her to do."

Marani was too well trained to object, though she seemed distressed. Kira knew Marani would never reveal what had happened here. The slave quickly stripped the vac-suit from her sweaty body and disappeared to perform her task.

Kira dressed herself, knowing she needed to collect her wits and make sure she had an impeccable witness to testify to her presence on the *Siren's Song* at the time of death, just in case she had accidentally left some evidence behind on New Hope. She would be meeting up with Worf tomorrow in the Zakdorn system, and everyone knew that it was impossible to cross the light-years between Betazed and Zakdorn in one day.

Placing the portal in the special blue case she had ordered to protect it, Kira opened the panel vault. She put the case inside with a lingering caress. The ancient artifact made her wishes come true. She locked it away securely.

Then she glanced at the closed door to the 'fresher. Seven had been in there for nearly twelve standard hours, and was probably fairly hungry by now. Kira knew she would have to do something about Seven. The Terran had betrayed her as surely as Deanna had.

Kira had noticed how much time Seven was spending with B'Elanna. She had even ordered one of her slaves to record Seven's interactions with B'Elanna during their tours. It was clear that Seven had become close to B'Elanna. In order to find out whether Seven was still loyal to Kira, she had devised a plan to ask Seven to kill B'Elanna. If Seven protested and didn't lie about her feelings for B'Elanna, Kira had intended to ask Seven to kill Deanna Troi. Surely Seven could have no qualms about that.

Instead, Seven had lied. She obviously would rather be with B'Elanna than her. All Terrans were alike, sticking to their own feeble kind.

But she had a way to deal with that. Seven knew too much sensitive information about Winn Adami and the Overseer's job to go free.

Wearing her black skin-suit and donning her regal headband, Kira refused to think about Troi lying in her quarters in New Hope. She had always been good at putting nasty things out of her mind. Soon the memory would seem like a story she had once read, shocking and titillating, but nothing to do with her.

Humming, she left the inner sanctum, feeling better for the first time since her visit to the Betazed system.

Kira discovered that Seven had set up quite an efficient Overseer system. She was soon able to locate the shipping schedules and find a slave ship that supplied mining colonies in the nearby sectors. Along with a few other inconsequential things, Kira told the commander of the *Siren's Song* to order the slave ship to rendezvous with them en route to Zakdorn.

Several hours later, the Pakled slave trader appeared on her screen in the office. The Pakled seemed impressed by Kira's position and bearing. His mouth hung open slackly in a grin, and he kept idiotically repeating, *"Whatever you want, just name it."*

It was very flattering and as it should be.

"I have a slave I don't want any longer." Kira avoided looking directly at the Pakled. His hairy brows and vacant expression repulsed her. "Perhaps you have a pleasure slave you could trade for her, under the table? I don't want this transaction recorded."

"What's wrong with her?" The Pakled's high, whiny voice was irritating. He never stopped grinning.

"She was a worker in the Bajoran ore refinery when I picked her up. Her beauty attracted me, but she is belligerent and dangerous. I've had her locked up for most of my journey, but I don't want to take her back to Bajor to contaminate my slave population."

"Okay," the Pakled replied. *"We might have a pleasure slave. His price is higher than a mine worker."*

"I'll throw in two strips of latinum," Kira told him.

The Pakled wasn't smiling anymore, obviously wary of such generosity. *"You hate her so much, why not toss her out an airlock?"*

Kira pressed her lips together in distaste at such a blunt proposal. Killing Troi had been bad enough, was she reduced to putting down all of her betrayers by her own hand? "Her arrogance offends me. She's Terran, yet thinks she isn't a slave. She also lied to me, and I want her punished. I want her to know she is a slave, and was never anything but a slave, until she dies a slave's death."

The Pakled didn't seem very interested. *"Okay"* was all he said.

"Good, I'll have her delivered to your ship shortly." Kira paused, glancing at the screen. "Oh, by the way, the Terràn is mute. I was forced to silence her one day, and the job was done too well. I don't suppose that will be a problem?"

The Pakled's expression fell. He had been intending to question Seven, an obvious desire considering the slave had been in the Overseer's possession. That was why Kira had taken the precaution of having Seven's vocal cords biomechanically locked.

"Who listens when a slave talks?" the Pakled commander asked rhetorically.

"Good. Marani will handle the exchange."

Kira ended transmission and called up the view of the Pakled ship. It carried over five hundred slaves in its bulbous hold, and appeared likely to fall apart when it went to warp. Seven could be beamed on board directly from the 'fresher, and there would be no record in the *Siren's Song* computer to indicate they had met the Pakled ship. At the next port she would log Seven off the ship, and that's where the Terran would apparently disappear. It was much cleaner than pushing Seven out an airlock . . . and there was no risk that one of her crew might talk about it.

Kira's ship arrived in the Zakdorn system a day later and was challenged by armada vessels. The commander of the *Siren's Song* woke Kira to inform her that the Alliance Armada was in battle mode and wouldn't let them into the system.

It took Kira some time to get hold of the *Negh'Var* and obtain clearance from one of the senior officers. She intended to make someone pay for this indignity.

Soon they entered synchronous orbit around the eighth planet, near the *Negh'Var*. The other armada vessels were dispersed through the system on battle alert.

Kira locked herself in Seven's former office to make the call to Worf. She preferred not to have an audience during that all-important moment when she would be told the terrible news.

The woolly black head of Worf's First Officer appeared on the screen. Koloth's eyes were red with battle rage.

"I will not be kept waiting!" Kira exclaimed imperiously. "I want standing orders that the *Siren's Song* is never to be detained."

First Officer Koloth had never made a secret of his dislike for Kira. He didn't even respond to her command. *"The Regent Worf is unavailable to speak to you. We are preparing to depart immediately."*

"We, who's we? I just got here."

"The armada is leaving." Koloth sneered. *"It matters not what you do."*

"I won't take this insolence!" Kira shouted. "Get Worf *now.*"

"Impossible." His teeth showed. *"Perhaps you haven't heard . . . the Regent's companion has been killed by an Andorian strike team."*

Kira hesitated, letting her mouth fall open in imitation

of the Pakled commander. Too bad all her practice was being wasted on Koloth. "Deanna?"

"The Regent prepares now to extract revenge."

Kira took several deep breaths. "But it can't be true. How? I left Deanna only last week on New Hope."

"Security was faulty," Koloth said shortly, examining a padd someone handed him. *"We are leaving orbit now."*

"I'm going with you."

"The Siren's Song *is not part of the armada,"* the first officer pointed out.

Kira leaned closer. "Just try and stop me."

She signed off and gave the orders to the commander of the *Siren's Song* to follow the armada—at a safe distance. She didn't want to be involved in this mess, but she certainly needed to stay close to Worf. Soon he would appear and she would be there to comfort him.

Chapter 14

SEVEN CROUCHED IN the holding tank on board the slave ship, crowded by dozens of Terrans. Many cried or wailed, a continuous din of loss and confusion. The smell was sickening, with grime clinging to the slimy metal decks and walls, smearing her skin and hair until she was just as blackened and fetid as everyone else.

Every day the Pakled handlers brought in a tub of nutrient sticks, beating back the hungry slaves and dragging off the ones who had died. Despite her superior physical abilities, Seven found it difficult to grab a bland nutrient stick. Though there were young children in the hold, there was no semblance of order. It was as if they were feral animals, occasionally turning on each other and attacking using their teeth and nails. The desperate shrieks were heartrending during a fight as legs and arms hopelessly flailed.

Seven couldn't speak because Kira had placed a bio-mechanical lock on her vocal cords. She mostly crouched next to a structural I-beam, hoping her implant could repair the damage. It might take weeks to break the bonds on the chemical lock and restore mobility. She might never regain full use of her voice.

Her situation was desperate, more desperate than any-thing she had ever encountered. But she knew that if she could hold on, the Obsidian Order would track her down and retrieve her. Her cranial implant database was in-valuable, containing everything she had learned about Kira and the Alliance. Surely Tain would make every ef-fort to retrieve her implant.

But as the days blended into one another, always dark and mostly sleepless because of the noise, Seven grew weaker. She began to doubt the Obsidian Order could find her. The Pakled handlers shifted a large number of slaves in and out of the hold almost every day, and pre-sumably a ship this size had many holds full of Terrans. None of the slaves had an identifying mark or number, indeed those who were once marked now bore a black lasered bar obscuring it. They were anonymous fodder for the unregistered market.

Seven knew she should get off the slave ship. The more stops they made, the harder it would be for Tain to find her. The next time the Pakleds came in, grinning as they kicked Terrans out of their way, she edged forward into the weak shaft of light shining through the hatch.

"You!" The Pakled handler pointed at a group of three women. His hairy brows stuck straight up in the middle of his forehead, but otherwise he looked like a jovial baby with a voice to match. "Take them. And that one," he added, pointing to a sniveling young man next to Seven. "The Sol mining camps don't care what they get."

Seven's head jerked up at the name of the system. She thrust herself in front of the young man, moving toward the handler in a crouch. Whenever a slave tried to stand up, they were mercilessly beaten back by the handlers.

"You want to go?" the Pakled asked, confused.

Seven remained where she was, blocking the young man. He was so weak that he would probably die in an asteroid mining complex. She could survive anything, and Sol was the center of the Alliance. From there, she might be able to contact B'Elanna.

"Take her," the Pakled ordered, laughing now. "She's stupid enough."

Seven was dragged into an ancient shuttle along with some other Terrans from the holds. Next to her was a pale woman with long bedraggled hair. This close, Seven could see it was red, brighter than Kira's hair. "Anything to get out of there," the Terran breathed in relief, sliding down against the wall next to Seven.

Seven nodded, keeping an eye on the Pakleds who were arguing about the trajectory to the mining complex. She couldn't see through the port, but she wished she could get a glimpse of Sol.

"I'm Beverly Crusher," the slave told Seven.

Seven gestured to her throat and shook her head to indicate she couldn't speak.

A spark of interest leaped in Beverly's eyes. "Is it natural? Or did they do something to you?"

Seven nodded, making a slashing motion across the base of her neck.

"I'm a healer," Beverly said, reaching out to touch Seven's throat.

Seven jerked back, bumping into the Terran next to her. He cried out, mostly in fear. A Pakled shouted, "Keep it down back there!"

Beverly pulled away, disappointed and humiliated. "I don't blame you. I *was* a healer, on the Deneva colony, but I couldn't . . . there was nothing I could do about the plague . . ."

Beverly started to cry without making a sound, her head sagging to her knees. Seven tried to ignore her, listening to the muttered commands of the Pakleds up front, memorizing the movements of the shuttle to determine the line of approach to the mining station. It was standard procedure for Obsidian agents.

Yet she was distracted by the woman doctor. She wondered what it had been like for Beverly, living on a colony among other Terrans. She wanted to ask if they were slaves, and how she became a healer, but her voice didn't work.

Seven looked at the other Terrans, some dazed beyond feeling or thought, others so frightened they were shaking and wild-eyed. She could feel her own skin caked in the filth of the slaveship. Yet even blackened with space dust, they each were very different. Why did people say that Terrans looked alike? Every one had a life before they were brought here. They were jerked from their existence, and thrown away like the dregs of the galaxy.

The shuttle locked on to the mining complex with a clank and scrape as the airlocks met. Seven lifted her chin, trying not to hunch her shoulders as they were shoved through the airlock. The Pakleds were arguing behind them as new handlers took over; Klingons with pain sticks.

The Klingons drove the Terrans down a long tube enclosed by wire mesh, then into a cylindrical room where they were ordered to disrobe. Laughing, the Klingons made a few of the Terrans gather the clothes and stick them into an airlock. Seven tried not to care that she was naked, but it was impossible. Then the Klingons withdrew and the end of the cylinder clanked shut.

"They'll open the airlock!" one of the men shrieked. The sound of twisting metal silenced their yells. Seven took one last deep breath, looking at the airlock like the others, waiting . . . then they were blasted from every side by ion jets. Her chest was compressed under the pressure, making her lungs empty with a rush.

After a few moments, she realized she was on her hands and knees, choking and coughing, trying to regain her breath. It was ugly but efficient. She was shining clean, including her teeth.

Then the Klingons were back, opening the end of the cylinder and prodding them out. Seven grabbed a few gauze rags from the pile outside the door. She quickly tied one around her hips and crossed the other two over her chest. Her boots were gone along with the rest of her clothes, but the grate decking was warm from the engines.

In a daze, she tried to assess the construction to determine what sort of space station it was, but her comparative database didn't seem to be working. She was distracted by the sound of scraping metal and the faint yells echoing up the tubes or from the bays they passed. She felt cold though she knew it was warm in the corridor, too warm. Sweat was running down her neck and forehead. She wanted to run.

The Klingons opened a bay door, shoving the Terrans into a long corridor. The man in front of her screamed as a Klingon poked him with a pain stick. He hurried through a narrow hatch next to the Klingon. Seven moved too quickly to be caught, diving through after him. Then, as suddenly as everything had happened, the hatch closed and she was in a dark hole again, surrounded by the gray faces of Terrans, moaning and suffering and torn from everything they knew.

The holding cell on the mining complex was long and narrow, barely tall enough for Seven to walk between the double row of cots. There were twelve cots, and she felt each one until she found an empty space on the top row. The first night was so similar to the seven days on the slave ship that she almost regretted getting off. But it was a relief to have her own place to lie down and to finally feel clean again.

She actually got some sleep that night and woke to a loud buzz. The others moved so fast that Seven was the last one through the hatch and into the corridor. It was filled with Terrans, pushing and shoving. They carried Seven along with them.

When she stumbled and almost fell, someone caught her arm and pulled her up. It was a Vulcan woman. Seven barely caught sight of her verdant skin and pointed ears among the faces of the other slaves.

"They open the airlocks at the end of each holding cell," the Vulcan told her, pulling her along. "Anything or anyone left behind is blown into space."

Seven thought that was a good reason for haste. Soon she lost the Vulcan in the stream of people, but it reminded her of the Vulcan twins Kira was so fond of. They had never spoken a word in her hearing. Why hadn't she ever considered what they might tell her?

The mining slaves poured into the bay where rows of Augmented Personnel Modules hung from launching rods. The battered APMs had two flexible arms attached to an inverted teardrop vehicle. It was big enough for one person to stand inside. The bubble top was made of clear plasteel to offer maximum visibility.

Like the others, Seven stepped inside an APM, grasping the handles that moved the arms. The door automatically shut, squeezing her feet together and pushing her into the front panel. Her head and shoulders filled the bubble top.

Suddenly her APM jerked and swung out, one in a string of twelve tugged by an automated buoy. There were no controls inside her module other than the arm operators, and she couldn't see what kept her tethered to the other APMs. Most likely a tractor beam was being emitted from the automated buoy.

As they pulled away from the mining complex, heading for the first jagged boulders of the asteroid ring, she could finally see the mining station. It reminded her of the shipyards of Utopia Planitia. The brown metal structure was curiously smooth yet segmented in distinctive Terran construction. The asteroid mines were another ancient remnant of the Terran race, once worked by slaves her people had gathered from across the galaxy. Now the mining complex was used to hold Terran slaves who worked the rich asteroid ring. Nothing really changed, only the names.

That was what Seven learned her first day in the mines. She copied what the other APMs were doing, hundreds of strings of them attached to different-colored buoys. Everything was in multiples of twelve, a number which must hold some ancient Terran significance.

Her buoy was red, as were the others in her launching bay. Their buoy circled the APMs around an asteroid, and Seven spent the day splitting off chunks. The weak lasers at the end of her segmented arm units sliced through the mineral rock. The burn marks on the other modules showed where a laser had missed the rock and struck one of the APMs. Seven wondered how many slaves they lost that way. Some of the burns looked almost deep enough to pierce the armor plating.

Her cranial implant told her that twelve Sol hours passed while they worked. She could stop as long as she wanted to, but it was boring just standing there. Meanwhile the buoy gathered the loose chunks into a force-field net attached to the last module. At the end of the day, it dragged the APMs back to the mining complex. The rocks were taken away by another buoy, while their APM string returned to the launching bay. They passed through the pressurized forcefield and landed on the launch arms. The APM was still swinging slightly as the doors on the module popped open.

On her way out of the bay, Seven gathered several nutrient sticks from a ledge next the corridor. Then there was a scramble for beds in the holding cells closest to the launching bay, with Seven ending up near the middle.

Every day was the same after that. They never saw the Klingon handlers. The slaves were always alone, going out to the asteroid fields, burning off rocks, coming back to eat and sleep together before returning to the solitude of the asteroid fields. She saw people blown into space every morning, for moving too slowly or being too sick to get up from their cots. The modules went out, and came back to the same launching bay in a monotonous danger-filled routine.

Seven soon noticed that certain groups of people stayed together. They chose the same string of APMs and they slept in the same holding cell. No one disputed such organized behavior. Seven yearned to enter one of these select groups. Surely if anyone had contact outside this slave bay, it would be them.

The most organized group was led by a mature woman with steady eyes and a no-nonsense manner. Her brown hair had reddish highlights, reminding Seven of the doctor, Beverly Crusher. The worn and faded doctor was among the shuffling dead now, fighting with blank eyes to get her nutrient sticks and joining the mindless rush through the corridors.

But this other Terran woman was vital and strong. She led her crew by example, and they clearly took pride in themselves as a team. Seven wondered what happened in their holding cell when it was sealed for sleep shift. She tried to get in the APM string behind theirs, so she could return before them and linger to watch when they returned from their work shift.

Her efforts paid off one day when their string returned to the bay, and there was a commotion as one of them was unloaded from the APM, dead. A slipped laser had pierced the bubble of the APM. Several of them had tears running down their cheeks, but they moved quickly. While two went to gather their nutrient bars and several secured a holding cell, the others carried their dead comrade to the ledge where sick or dead slaves were sometimes placed. Most were simply left in their cot or APM to be blown into space, but these Terrans showed respect for their fallen friend.

Seven hurried after the two who went to secure the cell. But they wouldn't let her in. Even after the others returned, they refused to move out of the way. She couldn't force them to accept her. And she couldn't explain herself because she had no voice.

Taking a cot in a holding cell near theirs, Seven was ready in the morning, waiting at the hatch when it opened. Instantly she joined the running group, shoving people aside in her haste. The corridor quickly filled, but Seven refused to give an inch. She managed to jump into an APM in their string. With all twelve filled, the doors closed and they were off.

Their faces were indistinct in the dark modules, but Seven knew they were watching her. She was careful to keep her lasers pointed away from the other APMs, using them with dexterity to prove she was not a risk to the others. She watched constantly for drift, bracing herself and shutting off the lasers whenever she bumped into another APM.

Seven also worked steadily. It was not much, but it was all she could do. She was certain there was a way to cull slaves who did not perform the job adequately.

When their buoy returned to the launching bay, Seven followed the group to the holding cell they had chosen. Two Terrans were guarding the door; a strong man with dark skin, and the leader with her reddish-brown hair falling over her forehead. Seven silently waited, asking for entry with her eyes.

"Don't you have anything to say for yourself?" the woman demanded, rough yet not unkindly.

Seven shook her head, cutting her hand across her throat.

The woman's eyes softened. "You can't speak?"

Seven made a rasping noise, the best she could do right now. It was better than nothing, which meant the implant was slowly making progress in repairing the damage.

Their eyes were skeptical, so Seven did the only thing

she could do. She scratched her thigh with her finger-nail, bracing herself against the pain and knowing the implant would kick in if it got bad enough. With several quick swipes, she drew a dark line of blood.

"What are you doing?" exclaimed the dark man in concern. He tried to stop her, but the leader blocked his hand. "Chakotay, let's see what she has in mind."

Seven pointed to herself, then carefully drew a number "7" on the hatch. Then she pointed to herself again.

"You're Seven?" the leader asked curiously.

Seven nodded vigorously, then leaned down to scratch herself again. She would plead her case in blood, and surely they would let her join them.

The leader glanced at Chakotay, who was looking even more concerned. "You've convinced me," he told Seven, stopping her hand as she began to draw more blood.

The leader stepped aside to let Seven into the holding cell. "You don't have to hurt yourself any more, Seven. I'm Kathryn Janeway and this is Chakotay. Come in and meet the rest of my crew."

That night Seven felt as if she had climbed from a bottomless pit back into some form of humanity. The low voices of the Terrans discussed things of importance near the front of the cell, while two others kept an eye on Seven in the rear bunk. The fact that they had things to talk about was enough to reassure Seven that her situation was not hopeless. They even hung a privacy drape between the rest of the holding cell and the sanitation unit, a small airlock under the main one. After her near-animal state, Seven was almost overcome with gratitude.

On subsequent nights, from things Seven overheard, she realized that Andor had been utterly decimated by Worf's armada. It was generally believed that an Andorian strike team had killed his companion, Deanna Troi. In revenge, Worf was slaughtering every Andorian in Alliance territory.

Seven was certain that it hadn't been Andorians. Kira must have killed Troi using the Iconian portal. It was just like Kira to plant evidence to implicate someone else. But Seven couldn't tell anyone. Her croaking words made the others shake their heads in confusion, and they refused to let her draw blood to write notes. She could only listen to them, wondering how they had heard everything. At least it proved they had contact with the outside.

Seven had to wait for her vocal cords to heal, laboring diligently during their work shift, and staying out of everyone's way at night. She tried to win their respect. Then she discovered one line of communication out of the slave bays.

That night the lights didn't go out as usual. Instead, banging and yelling echoed in the corridor. Janeway's crew was tense. Chakotay stayed close to a teenaged girl, while the Vulcan woman was speaking softly to a thin man who was chewing his lip. Seven had been learning their names and characters. The thin man, Paris, was usually either angry or in despair. The girl called Robin clung to anyone who would let her, while Chakotay always kept one eye on Janeway. Selar, the

Vulcan who had helped Seven the first day in the corridor, was a devotee of Spock. Seven thought Spock and his message of peace should be an object of scorn for everyone who was reduced to this terrible state. Yet Janeway's crew spoke reverently about his words and referred to him as the Prophet.

A blinding light shone into the holding cell as the hatch was flung open. Janeway led the way with her crew right on her heels. Harry Kim, a young man with a round friendly face and surprisingly easygoing temper, urged Seven to hurry. That's when she realized Kim had been assigned to help her, just like Chakotay was making sure Robin was doing okay.

Klingons with pain sticks were standing in the corridor, ushering several holding cells of Terrans to the massive bay door. Passing through, she recognized the patterns of I-beams and the mesh enclosure of the main corridor. The Klingons weren't as vicious with the pain sticks this time as the slaves filed into the cylindrical ion chamber.

Seven covered her eyes, prepared for the ion blast. This time, they were allowed to keep their rags on. The gauze did nothing to stop the removal of debris and bacteria from their skin and hair, yet preserved a bit of dignity. Under the ion bombardment, the red infected cut on her arm caused by a ragged APM panel sealed over and faded to a faint pink. The scabbed scratches on her thigh disappeared completely.

As Seven left the decontamination chamber, with Kim sticking close to her elbow, she noticed that Janeway was standing next to the Klingons. Even wearing rags, she appeared to be their equal. Her arms were crossed and shoulders squared. The Klingons grudgingly spoke to her. One of them was swinging his pain stick as if he was bored.

Kim urged Seven away before she could hear more than a few words about "shift changes." They were herded back to their holding cell. After nearly an hour, the lights went off, and the routine recommenced. As diverting as it was, Seven did not think it was a likely avenue of escape.

The next break came after a few duty shifts, when Seven noticed Janeway examining an APM that had suffered laser fire across the lower node. Seven didn't want Kim pulling her away again, so she ducked behind an APM while the others left the launching bay. Janeway stayed even after the last buoy had landed and the zombie slaves had rushed back to their holding cells.

Several times Seven had observed what took place in the launching bay, but she always stayed near the hatch to the corridor. Her original plan to reprogram a buoy and steal it to drive an APM was abandoned when she realized the launching bay was depressurized during their sleep shift.

Uneasy, she wondered when Janeway would return to the safety of the corridor. Seven finally took a step forward to remind her that depressurization would occur soon. Then she saw Terrans in work jumpers approaching the APMs. Several Terran workers wrestled a damaged APM forward using antigrav units. Two others greeted Janeway, bending to discuss the damage to the APM she was examining.

Surprised, Seven leaned out to watch as the Terran workers dragged several damaged APMs through a doorway that had opened in the side of the launching bay.

"Hey! What are you doing here?" a worker demanded, grabbing Seven's arm from behind. "Get back to your holding cell."

Janeway turned. "That's okay, Jerem. She's one of my crew." She went back to speaking to the other workers.

Jerem snorted at Seven, giving her the once-over, before stalking away. She had never felt disdain from a Terran before.

Then Janeway joined her and they started back through the APMs toward the corridor of holding cells. Janeway told Seven, "I used to work in the maintenance bays. I'm an engineer by training."

Seven had to force herself to speak. It was now or never. "Why . . ." she struggled, her voice cracked and husky. "You here?"

"Oh, so you can finally speak," Janeway said, stopping just outside the corridor to the holding cells. "What happened to you?"

"A Bajoran . . ." Seven added a silent cutting motion across her throat, then shrugged to indicate it had been poorly done. "You?"

Janeway sighed. "You've seen the APMs, they need to be overhauled or replaced. We're losing dozens of people every day because of equipment failure. I must have talked too loudly about it, because I ended up in here."

Seven wanted to know how long Janeway had endured the slave bay. She wanted to know if she would ever rise to the status of a maintenance worker again. But Seven's curiosity was nothing compared to her need to get out.

"I need help," Seven whispered.

"Don't we all?" Janeway pointed out.

Seven realized she had nothing to offer but the truth. "I worked for the Overseer. She tried to silence me."

Janeway stared at her, then slowly started to smile. "You know, I thought I'd heard them all. . . . You work for the Overseer."

Seven swallowed, her throat burning. "Must get . . . message to B'Elanna."

"The Intendant of Sol?" Janeway let out a harsh laugh. "I'll put in a call to her right now."

Seven put her hand to her throat, ignoring the terrible pain that urgently told her to stop. "You have contacts."

"I have no reason to risk their lives or mine for you." Janeway turned down the corridor. Chakotay was waiting at the hatchway to their holding cell, his brows drawn together curiously.

"I'm one . . . of your crew," Seven insisted. Janeway hesitated, just as Seven was hit by an endorphin wave. She went light-headed as her implant compensated for the pain of speaking.

Seven took several deep breaths, trying to center herself in spite of the euphoria. At least now the pain wouldn't stop her. She had a chance to convince Janeway. "You've shown me how to be Terran. What makes us more than slaves."

Janeway glanced at her, interested in spite of herself. "What is that?"

"Determination," Seven admitted roughly. She thought of the miracles of destruction she had accomplished for Enabran Tain. Why? Because she had nothing else to live for. "I can help you and your crew."

Janeway narrowed her eyes, as if trying to see inside Seven. Seven didn't flinch. She meant every word she said. Her only hope was that B'Elanna would care enough to come get her.

"Please." Seven found it difficult to say. But she remembered Winn Adami, and knew it had to be done. She had to make restitution. "Tell B'Elanna I'm here. For your crew. For all Terrans."

Janeway briefly frowned, but she took Seven's arm. As she ushered her down the corridor, the decompression lights began to flash in the launching bay. "I'll see what I can do, Seven."

Chapter 15

B'ELANNA WAS IN a foul mood, and she was certain that things would never get better. First Duras, now Deanna Troi . . . it was enough to send her into everlasting battle rage. It had nearly destroyed Worf.

B'Elanna was alone, and felt as if she had lost every friend, including Worf. The *Sitio* had traveled at top warp speed to join the Alliance Armada on the eve of the Great Andorian Massacre, a clash of vessels that had surely sent Deanna victorious to *Sto'Vo'Kor.* In her name, Worf had utterly destroyed the Andorian civilization, rendering the three planets in their system lifeless.

Then Worf had retreated into solitude, behavior uncharacteristic of a Klingon. She had seen him only once since the Great Andorian Massacre. Everyone had hoped he would purge his rage in the fight, and he had been vital and energized while the outcome was uncertain. He had roared as he killed the Andorian Intendant while his homeworld burned down below. Afterward, Worf became sullen and unresponsive.

B'Elanna took an angry swipe at the holographic "enemy" in the exercise program. They were back at Utopia Planitia, with the *Sitio* in dock while the Regent's flagship orbited Mars. Worf had ordered the other armada vessels to disburse on patrols to track down the last Andorians.

Everything should have returned to normal. But it didn't. She was practicing alone, bereft of even Seven's company. She had truly enjoyed working out with Seven. They were so evenly matched.

B'Elanna had contacted the *Siren's Song* soon after joining the armada, looking for Seven. But Seven was gone, reportedly disappearing on the busy spaceport of Tellar. Kira had bitterly denounced Seven. She said the Terran had "deserted" her shortly before she had rendezvoused with Worf in Zakdorn.

B'Elanna thought it was strange Seven hadn't contacted her. So did the Cardassians who had been sent looking for Seven on behalf of Ghemor, her foster father. The big news in the Alliance was that Ghemor had replaced Natima Lang as head of the Detapa Council. Among other things, Ghemor wanted to find Seven. But Kira's crew and logs reported exactly the same thing, that Seven had left the *Siren's Song* at Tellar.

With a vicious growl, B'Elanna decapitated one of her "enemies." Kira was not invulnerable. Yet her investigation of the Winn Adami assassination confirmed that a

Cardassian, Tora Ziyal, had killed the First Minister. Ziyal was linked to Gul Dukat, who had been censured by the Cardassian government for some classified reason. Everything pointed to Cardassia rather than Kira, so B'Elanna gave up trying to link Kira with Duras's death. She had finally closed the investigation into Duras's death when Worf told her that the rumors on Qo'noS were that K'mpec had hired the assassin. K'mpec's house was in ruins.

So B'Elanna had been concentrating on getting rid of Kira. Over the past several weeks, she had secretly obtained the agreement of every major Intendant and scores of minor Intendants and Alliance officials. They wanted Kira to be replaced. Some were even prepared to disrupt trade to make their point.

As it turned out, they didn't have to. Kira's abuses were bad enough, but now the smooth-running system was fast deteriorating. Conflicting shipping schedules were issued, deliveries were delayed or went missing, and production levels fell short in almost every Alliance facility. Food supplies from the colonies were increasingly irregular.

It was only a matter of time before everything fell apart. B'Elanna figured Seven had created a management structure that needed intelligent monitoring. Kira was obviously incapable of that.

At this point, B'Elanna would have told Worf that Seven had been performing the Overseer's job rather than Kira, but she never saw Worf. She wasn't sure what good it would do anyway. The *Siren's Song* was once again wedged into the *Negh'Var*'s largest docking bay, by order of the Overseer. Kira was entrenched in her position.

"Intendant?" her Klingon aide asked, apparently unsure whether B'Elanna had completed the practice simulation.

B'Elanna realized she was just standing there holding the knife in one slack hand. "End program," she ordered. "What is it?"

Her newest aide was an up-and-coming young Klingon who reminded B'Elanna of herself ten years ago. "I've heard something interesting. I don't know if it's true, but the supply shuttle pilot for the mining complex says that Seven is there. She's in one of the slave bays."

B'Elanna shook her head. "Seven? Here in Sol? That's impossible."

"He says Seven sent you a message. She needs your help."

B'Elanna sheathed her knife, thinking quickly. "Is each bay monitored?"

"Yes, but the tapes only go back twenty standard days."

"That should be enough. I want you to personally look at the tape for each bay for the past several days."

"There's over forty bays on that mining complex," the aide said doubtfully. "It will take forever."

"Use your brain," B'Elanna ordered. "Watch the shift changes. Seven is not your typical Terran. If she's there, it shouldn't be too hard to spot her."

"I'll have the tapes sent right away," the aide agreed.

"Go!" B'Elanna ordered, giving the aide a shove. "I want a report by this afternoon."

B'Elanna smiled for the first time in weeks, as her

aide hurried to begin her search. If Seven was in the Sol system, B'Elanna would find her.

"Here's another view," the aide said to B'Elanna, switching the image on the computer screen.

B'Elanna examined the flat image, noting the woman's high cheekbones and cleft chin. She also had shining white-blond hair, unusual even for Terrans. She stood head and shoulders above most of the other shuffling slaves.

"That's Seven, all right."

The aide consulted the tape. "She's in the Delta slave bay."

"How'd she get there?" B'Elanna mused, staring at the image.

"I can requisition the delivery documents," the aide offered, pleased that she had been successful.

"Don't bother," B'Elanna told her. "Get the runabout ready." No need to alert everyone by taking the *Sitio* out. The mining complex was only an hour away by full impulse. She could get there and back without anyone being the wiser. "Sign it out yourself. I'll meet you in the docking bay."

B'Elanna's last inspection of the mining complex had been some time ago. The supervisor seemed to have things well in hand, though there was a relatively high labor turnover.

B'Elanna waited while her aide went with the Klingon handlers down to the Delta bay to fetch Seven. It was

Delta's sleep shift, fortunately, otherwise she would have to wait for the entire bay of APMs to return from the asteroids. Utopia Planitia's construction yards required the large quantities of raw material provided by the asteroid fields. They couldn't afford to give up the tonnage gathered by one slave bay.

Impatiently B'Elanna waited in the supervisor's office, while the Klingon valiantly tried to ply her with bloodwine and rejoice over the Great Andorian Massacre. B'Elanna wasn't in the mood. At this point she doubted that Seven was here. It seemed too good to be true.

But when the door opened, her beaming aide brought in Seven. The Terran didn't have much on, and she hesitated when she saw B'Elanna. Seven's fists clenched and her lips tightened, the only sign of emotion she would show to the roomful of people. "B'Elanna," she said in a rough voice.

B'Elanna couldn't help giving her a sly smile, alluding to her attire, "Looks like the old Seven."

"Never again," Seven said grimly. B'Elanna was impressed by the way she coolly regarded everyone in the room. She could have been the Empress of Romulus, rather than a ragged, barefoot slave.

"Nice to have you back," B'Elanna told her.

Chapter 16

ONCE SEVEN WAS on board B'Elanna's runabout, on course to Utopia Planitia, she replicated an enveloping cloak to cover herself. She didn't intend to be recognized. B'Elanna's Klingon aide was flying the runabout, and they told Seven that no one else knew she was here. It had taken days, but somehow Janeway had gotten word to B'Elanna via the supply pilot. Seven silently affirmed that she would not forget Janeway.

It took nearly the entire trip to Mars for Seven to convince B'Elanna that stealth was necessary. She explained how Kira had sold her to the Pakleds, who had then sold her to the Sol asteroid mining complex as an unregistered slave. B'Elanna wasn't too happy about that, and she wanted to go right back and castigate the supervisor for buying unregistered slaves. That meant the labor shortages were higher than reported, and funds were being diverted that she didn't know about.

"Later, you can deal with the mining complex," Seven assured her. "I'm concerned about Kira."

"Who isn't?" B'Elanna retorted.

"I can force Kira to resign as Overseer."

"What?" B'Elanna asked incredulously. "How?"

A good agent revealed only the information that was necessary. B'Elanna would tell Worf if she knew that Kira had killed Deanna Troi. Then Seven's hold on Kira would be gone.

Seven needed access to real power. After her experience as a slave, she knew she could no longer rely on Enabran Tain to protect her. She must have known it for some time, but she couldn't admit it to herself. She had become a different person on this mission. She was Terran, not a slave, but a Terran like Janeway. She accepted the responsibility to help other Terrans, to live in cooperation and peace, and to make herself exist for more than death.

"Kira has something that I must get," she told B'Elanna.

"What?"

Seven couldn't tell anyone about the Iconian portal, not until she possessed it herself. With the portal in her possession, she could threaten to show it to Worf and reveal that Kira had killed Deanna Troi. Worf had ordered the death of every Andorian in the galaxy. What would he do to Kira?

"After I retrieve it," Seven told her, "I can convince Kira to step down as Overseer."

That got B'Elanna's attention. "Are you sure?" At Seven's nod, she eagerly asked, "What is it?"

"A weapon that Kira should have destroyed. It killed Winn Adami. If it was made public, it would cost Kira her power base in Bajor."

"Then Kira did kill Winn Adami! I knew it." B'Elanna's voice grew deadly. "Did she also kill Duras?"

"Duras? No." Seven was momentarily taken aback. Why was B'Elanna linking Winn Adami with Duras? She didn't want B'Elanna to discover that Seven herself had killed Duras.

B'Elanna seemed disappointed, but convinced. "It must have been K'mpec," she murmured. "So what do we do about Kira?"

"Where is the *Siren's Song?*" Seven asked.

"In the *Negh'Var* docking bay, of course," B'Elanna snorted. "Kira is waiting like an arachnid for Worf to come out."

"Good." It would be easier to gain access to the ship while it was inside the *Negh'Var.* "I need to go to the *Sitio* first to prepare."

"You'll be recognized when you board the *Negh'Var,*" B'Elanna pointed out.

"I can take care of that."

Her disguise wasn't surgical quality, but it was close. Seven had posed as a Klingon enough times to be able to pass.

She programmed the replicator for the proper prosthetics and a long wig of tangled black hair. When she darkened the rest of her skin, it looked fine. Donning the chest-exposing warrior's armor, she felt herself sliding into character despite the annoying weight of the prosthetics.

B'Elanna entered with a unimatrix tool to bond the edges of the prosthetics. She stopped short. "Seven?" She started to laugh. "I didn't recognize you."

Seven bared her teeth, showing the crooked dentures. "I am Zolat!"

"All right, all right," B'Elanna placated her. She passed the unimatrix over her forehead several times. Seven felt the prosthetic tighten, clenching her skin.

B'Elanna put the tool down. "Let's go, Zolat."

Seven piloted the runabout to the *Negh'Var*. By flying rather than transporting to the flagship, they would be in close proximity to Kira's ship. Seven downloaded the *Negh'Var* schematics when B'Elanna obligingly called them up, noting the location of the entrance to the immense docking bay.

Seven had flown Klingon ships before, and it was not difficult to pose as B'Elanna's pilot. The *Negh'Var* launch commander gave them clearance as if it were a routine occurrence. Seven landed near several shuttles, close to an airlock leading to the largest docking bay.

When the hatch opened, B'Elanna stepped outside to chat with the maintenance supervisor about some work they had done on the phaser banks of her runabout. Seven locked down the systems while B'Elanna told the supervisor that her little ship didn't need any work today.

As Seven stepped from the runabout, she instantly sensed the somber mood on the *Negh'Var*. As she and B'Elanna passed through the next few launching bays, Seven knew the difference must reflect the tone set by the Regent. She had been gathering the character of Zolat around her, anticipating that the Klingons would be riding a battle high from the recent Andorian massacre. But instead of victory, it seemed like they had been defeated. Worf must be truly suffering from the death of Deanna Troi.

B'Elanna was also subdued, yet her sharp gesture for Seven indicated her nervous excitement. Seven strode behind the Sol Intendant, following her into the docking bay that held the *Siren's Song*.

The *Siren's Song* stood eight decks high and nearly filled the bay from bow to stern. It was a fast yacht, meant for long-distance pleasure cruising. Now it was balanced on its slender landing gear in the dimly lit bay. Seven knew from their time on board the *Negh'Var* that the crew would rotate shifts with two at a time guarding the airlock inside the *Siren's Song*. Usually they played padd games or watched holonovels until they were relieved.

Seven slipped into the shadows near the *Siren's Song*'s airlock. B'Elanna went to the computer console in the corner of the docking bay and called the team through the comm. The airlock opened, and after a few moments two Bajorans settled their gold-braided uniforms as they hurried down the ramp into the bay. Kira had insisted that her crew get fancy outfits befitting her status as Overseer, but they hated the uncomfortable regalia.

With regret, Seven noted that Ro Laren was on duty. Ro was Bajoran but she had been kind to Seven, once offering her a jacket when she was shivering in a skimpy costume Kira had forced her to wear. But Seven didn't let regret stop her. B'Elanna drew the two crew members toward the computer panel in the bay wall, shocking them by insisting they move the *Siren's Song*. B'Elanna claimed the docking bay was needed for another cruiser that was coming off the shipyard scaffolds.

Seven slipped into the ship, as Ro protested that it would strain the *Siren's Song* to start the systems for a short flight only to shut everything down again. She tried to refer B'Elanna to her commander, but B'Elanna began to argue with them to give Seven time.

Seven soundlessly stepped down the corridor of the *Siren's Song* and climbed up two decks to Kira's quarters. The door to the common room remained closed, but when she placed her palm on the auto-sensor, it smoothly slid open. Kira had not canceled Seven's access, believing she was dying in a slave camp somewhere. It would be the last time Kira underestimated her.

Seven slipped through the common room into Kira's inner sanctum. She targeted the panel that held the Iconian portal, certain that Kira had left it on board. Most of her precious objects were still displayed on the *Siren's Song*, ready for a fast getaway. Clearly, Kira did not feel confident in her current situation.

Seven planted an explosive device on the panel vault, over the concealed locking mechanism. Ducking inside the 'fresher for safety, she remembered with a shudder the unpleasant hours she had spent inside prior to being sold as a slave. She triggered the explosive and the panel blew open. It made quite a noise, but Seven knew that nothing could penetrate Kira's soundproofed private quarters.

As the smoke rose, Seven was glad the ship's primary systems were off-line, otherwise the computer alert would have sounded. Waving aside the smoke, she saw the blue case that held the portal resting inside the vault. Kira was certainly a trusting soul.

Seven grabbed the portal, unconcerned about concealing the crime. She hoped to get away undetected, but now that she had the portal, she would not let it go.

Adrenaline raced through her body as she eased into the main corridor of the *Siren's Song*. The airlock was still open, and she could hear distant voices outside, arguing. Leaning into the airlock, she could see the two Bajorans facing away from her. Seven slipped out the airlock and back into the shadows, crouching behind the warp nacelle.

B'Elanna paused as if considering their words, and finally admitted, "I'll have to speak to your commander. But one way or another, the *Siren's Song* has to go."

B'Elanna probably meant every word. She would use this as an excuse to get rid of Kira, if she had to. Seven headed for the airlock to the adjacent bay, while Ro and her crewmate retreated in relief. Seven joined her after the crew members disappeared inside the *Siren's Song*.

"Did you get it?" B'Elanna asked as they returned to her runabout.

Seven held up the blue case. "Now Kira will step down."

"That's it?" B'Elanna asked curiously. She obviously thought it was a bloody knife.

"It's enough." Seven opened the hatch to the cruiser. She refused to let go of the portal. When they were seated at the controls, the portal in her lap, she turned to B'Elanna. "I will contact my foster father and ask the Detapa Council to back my appointment as Overseer."

B'Elanna's eyes widened. "You think he'll agree?"

"I know Ghemor will." Seven asked the real question. "But will the Klingons agree to appoint me Overseer?"

"I don't know . . . maybe if Worf supports you. Gowron would be willing to do anything for him right now."

"Would Worf support me?" Seven clenched her fist, feeling strong in the Klingon gear. "More to the point, would he back a Terran as Overseer?"

B'Elanna slowly shook her head. "He might. He vouched for me when I stood for Intendant."

"I would need your help," Seven told her.

B'Elanna grinned. "Why not? I'll never be appointed Overseer. I'm too Klingon. But I've got most of the Intendants ready to vote Kira out."

Seven finally smiled. "Then it *can* be done. We must return to the *Sitio* so I can call Ghemor."

Chapter 17

KIRA COULDN'T UNDERSTAND why Worf was being so difficult. All he had to do was come out and she could make him forget everything. But he stayed in the rooms he had shared with that devious empath . . . he never saw anyone, not even B'Elanna.

It was annoying.

Just when everything should have fallen into place, nothing was going right. The Intendants were avoiding her. Even the Alliance officials scattered whenever she appeared on Utopia Planitia. She didn't mind being feared, but she was a social person. What good was power if nobody flattered you?

She was bored with her Vulcan love slaves and even Marani couldn't please her. She missed Seven, and she wished she had not overreacted and cast her off. She had been crazed by that treacherous Betazoid and didn't know what she was doing.

Now she missed Seven's quiet beauty. Seven was highly ornamental for a Terran, always graceful and serene. Even more, Kira missed her management of the Overseer's duties. Everyone was complaining lately. The Vulcan she had acquired to perform Seven's job was inadequate, as was the Bajoran she had first hired. In a fit of remorse, Kira had even tried to track down the Pakled ship. But Seven had disappeared into the underground slave market as though she had never existed.

Oh well, Kira's motto was to focus on the good not the bad.

Kira clapped her hands for attention. "Marani, gather the last of those things, and have the boys help you take them to the *Siren's Song*."

Marani leaped to do her bidding, silently removing the few clothes and mementos Kira had brought onto the *Negh'Var*. The slaves loaded an antigrav cart and left.

Kira strolled through the spacious quarters, wishing the *Siren's Song* could afford such luxurious surroundings. But she would have to postpone her quest for a larger ship until her next visit to Utopia Planitia, when she would force B'Elanna to comply. There was a beautiful fifteen-deck ship that was almost completed, but Worf had vetoed her requisition order.

For now, she would take the *Siren's Song* from the *Negh'Var* docking bay. If that didn't summon Worf from his self-imposed isolation, then she would leave immediately for Bajor.

During the weeks of waiting for Worf to emerge, she had only discovered one possible method of gaining access to him. But that involved storming the door when First Officer Koloth arrived to give Worf the daily report. That method was too drastic for Kira's taste. She preferred to leave Alliance territory and let everything die down. Worf would come to her soon enough.

Her personal comm beeped. It was tied into the *Siren's Song,* by-passing the *Negh'Var's* communications grid. One of the *Siren's Song*'s Bajoran crew members said, *"Overseer? Navigator Ro, here. We have a problem."*

"What is it?" Kira demanded.

"Your quarters on the Siren's Song *have been broken into, and one of the sealed vaults has been destroyed."*

"Only one?" Kira asked, feeling a sudden chill. Not the Iconian portal . . .

"Yes. I don't know how it happened—"

"Order the crew to their stations," Kira interrupted. "I'll be right there."

Kira refused to believe the worst until she was standing in front of the empty vault with the panel hanging burnt and askew. It smelled awful in her quarters, as if something toxic had exploded into choking, sticky smoke.

The Iconian portal was gone. Marani was doing an inventory, but it appeared that nothing else was missing or had been touched. The outer door to her quarters had not been forced. The log indicated that the last person to access the quarters was Seven.

On questioning the guards, Kira discovered that B'Elanna had visited the docking bay not more than an hour ago, threatening to kick the *Siren's Song* off the flagship. Soon afterward, the guards thought they smelled smoke and investigated every deck.

Kira accessed the surveillance monitor in the launching bay, noting that two Klingons entered the bay. Only B'Elanna argued with the guards, while they stupidly left the airlock of the *Siren's Song* open.

So Seven and B'Elanna were working together against her.

Kira was in such a rage she could barely speak to the commander, ordering her to launch the *Siren's Song* immediately. It would take some time to power up the systems, but the commander murmured, "Yes, Overseer," before slinking off. She was responsible for the stupidity of her crew.

Kira paced back and forth in her inner sanctum, taunted by the wrecked vault, thinking of the tortures she could inflict on the two guards.

But that didn't solve her real problem. Seven could use the portal to kill her. Or she could show it to Worf and convince him that Kira had killed Deanna Troi.

Kira shivered at the thought of the Great Andorian Massacre. Worf had been magnificent and terrifying during the battle. Space had turned blue with Andorian bodies. She never wanted his wrath aimed at her.

But the Iconian portal proved nothing against her. Kira could say that Seven had stolen the portal from her weeks ago. Lately Kira had been spending more time with Deanna than Seven, so Seven had grown jealous of Deanna. Yes, that must be it. . . .

Kira had to get to Worf first. Glancing at the chrono, she realized that if she hurried, she might catch Koloth bringing the daily report to Worf's quarters. Without giving it another thought, she ran through the *Siren's Song*. She ignored her crew preparing to depart as she slipped out the airlock. She had to find the nearest turbolift.

Kira arrived just as First Officer Koloth was leaving. She rushed up as the door to Worf's quarters was sliding closed. "Wait!" Her leg got over the threshold to block the door. "Worf wants to see me."

Koloth was startled, and he tried to prevent her from entering. "Worf told me nothing about this."

"You don't know everything," Kira retorted, breathless and flustered. But she wasn't about to let a petty first officer get in her way. *"Move!* Or your Regent will hear about this."

She was the Overseer, after all, and Koloth reluctantly stepped aside.

Kira tossed her head as she shoved past the first officer, entering Worf's quarters. She hit the door command, shutting it in his face. Someday she would make Koloth pay for his insolence.

The quarters were darkened and empty. Kira remembered the time she and Worf had spent in these quarters when he used to visit Bajor. She checked the bedroom, but it was empty as well. Then she noticed a door at the other end of the main room. It was open, and when she stepped through, she was hit by the spicy scent of *sippis* flowers. Deanna had pointed them out on New Hope as her favorites.

The flickering flames of hundreds of candles cast the only light. Kira figured the computer alarm must have been permanently disabled to ignore the soot blackening the ceiling.

At the other end of the chamber was a shrine. The candles were massed against the wall beneath a shining re-curve sword. It had been hung with a sheer white scarf embroidered with tiny violets. Kira caught her breath, remembering the way Deanna had worn it over her hair as they toured Risa and later, Alpha Centauri.

Worf was kneeling in front of the altar, his head and shoulders bowed as if supporting a terrible weight. He was muttering something rapidly under his breath, and he braced himself with one hand to keep from falling forward into the flames.

Seeing him prostrate before the altar to his love, Kira was almost moved to pity. She had never seen such a display of adoration.

She knelt beside him. His eyes were red and bleary from lack of sleep as he turned his head. "Who dares to disturb me?"

"Worf," Kira softly exclaimed. Her hand reached out to touch his wild hair, but anger was building in his eyes.

"Don't push me away," she pleaded with him. "I miss her, too."

Worf's expression softened, and for a moment she wondered if a tear would fall. A Klingon warrior could cry?

"Deanna must have told you how close we were," Kira whispered. "We grew to be such good friends. More than friends . . ."

Worf took a deep breath, but he no longer seemed ready to cry.

"My loss is nothing compared to yours," Kira hastily added. "But surely we can comfort one another . . . I miss her so much . . ."

Worf turned away, kneeling in front of the draped sword. His head bowed and his lips began to move again.

"Worf!" Kira protested. Was the man made of stone? "You can't do this to yourself." When he continued to mutter, Kira added, "Deanna would hate to see you like this."

Worf whipped his head up. "I honor Deanna in the way she would have honored my death! For a month I will fast and hold vigil." His voice was hoarse from constant chanting.

Kira couldn't contradict him, not while he was glaring that way. Worf pushed her aside, looking up at the sword. "Be gone from here," he said before beginning his chant again.

"There are battles to be won, Worf." Kira refused to retreat, taking up a stance directly behind him. "People are trying to destroy our power, to sever the Regent from the Overseer. There are lies and rumors being spread . . ."

Worf continued his chanting.

Kira placed her hands on his broad shoulders, feeling

the hard armor. She leaned closer to his ear. "We must fight back. I can help you, just as *she* once helped you. In Deanna's name, I swear—"

Worf threw off her hands, roaring as he stood up, "You swear nothing in her name!"

"But Worf," she protested. "I only meant—"

Worf flung aside the low table, sending candles and hot wax flying through the air. Kira ducked and backed away as the rug began to smolder in several places.

"You know nothing of her!" Worf roared. His hands were clenched as he bore down on Kira.

She bolted to the nearest door. It swished open, and she rushed into the corridor.

Half-expecting Worf to follow, she was somewhat disappointed when the door simply closed behind her. It had been exciting for a moment, but now she wondered if she had made an irreparable mistake. Klingons were so touchy.

Straightening her foil headband, which had gotten knocked over one ear in her flight, Kira headed back down to the docking bay. It was definitely time for a strategic retreat.

Chapter 18

ENABRAN TAIN'S EYES continuously moved over the screens and readouts that encircled him in the command center of the Obsidian Order bunker. The slanted desk, surrounding screens, and ceiling monitors lined the small round room. It was deadly silent.

Yet monitoring the incoming data from thousands of agents planted across the galaxy took only one part of his brain. Mostly he was gloating over the latest news that had flashed by on the military bands. Gul Dukat had been demoted and assigned command of a military freighter.

It was a better denouement than Tain had anticipated. Dukat had exacerbated his situation by arrogantly refusing to bow to the general condemnation of his half-Bajoran daughter, Ziyal. The demotion came right on the heels of the censure by the Detapa Council because of his daughter's supposed involvement in the murder of the Bajoran First Minister. Dukat's mother announced that she disowned Dukat, and Dukat's wife had left him not long after Tain had introduced Ziyal to Cardassia. She took Dukat's other seven children with her.

Tain accessed the flight path of Dukat's freighter, watching its slow progress out of the Cardassia Prime system. He actually smiled at the thought of his fiercest enemy at the helm of the rickety ship, conveying replacement parts for environmental control units to one of Cardassia's colonies on the edge of the Beta Quadrant. That should keep him busy for a while. Dukat's manifest revealed that he had taken Ziyal with him, probably to keep Tain from getting his hands on her. But Tain didn't need Ziyal anymore. She had served her purpose, and it was unlikely that Dukat could recover his status again.

The Natima Lang project had also come to fruition. Tain had approved the appointment of Ghemor as head of the Cardassian Detapa Council, replacing Natima Lang. Ghemor would be a much more accommodating leader. Ghemor would expect concessions in return, yet that would allow Tain to gain some measure of control over him. Tain was continuously monitoring Ghemor's communications and had noted with approval that he was cautious in creating alliances or committing to specific legislature. Ghemor intended to solidify his position, likely with an eye to having as long a reign as Natima Lang's.

Tain was quite satisfied with the situation in Cardassia. As for the Alliance territories, the agents searching for Agent Seven had submitted negative reports thus far.

But it was only a matter of time. Their most promising lead was a Pakled slave ship whose flight path had crossed the *Siren's Song*'s. It could have rendezvoused with Kira's cruiser not long before they reached the Tellar system, where Seven had reportedly disembarked. His agents had thoroughly searched Tellar and were unable to find any report of a blond Terran who corresponded to Seven's holo-image. They were now searching each planet or station the Pakled ship had passed by, looking for Agent Seven.

Tain knew that after Seven was found and returned to him, her implant database would surely provide the information he needed to have influence on Kira. He had come very close with Agent Seven, but Garak's analysis had been fundamentally flawed. Kira would never respect a Terran enough to fall under her power.

As for Agent Seven, once her implant database was downloaded, she would be retrained. That would eliminate any glitches in her programming and restore his most prized agent to duty.

Perhaps Garak should be sent for retraining . . . it might shake him out of that staid routine he wallowed in. Logistically it could be done by having Garak "fall ill" of a unique Cardassian malady, requiring him to visit the homeland. Yet it could jeopardize his cover on Terok Nor if anyone detected the differences in his character after his return. Now more than ever, Tain needed someone on Terok Nor to watch Kira Nerys.

The flicker of an alert in a key area caught his attention. Using eye command, Tain lifted the transmission to the main screen. It was Ghemor's communications grid, activated by trigger words he had placed in the tap. He watched the transmission via split screen.

"Annika!" Ghemor exclaimed, looking both surprised and annoyed. "Where have you been?"

"That is irrelevant." Agent Seven's expression was severe as she faced the screen. Tain was in turmoil. Why would Agent Seven contact Ghemor instead of him?

On the other half of the screen, Ghemor frowned. Clearly he had never expected to see her again after she had disappeared from the Overseer's entourage.

Seven coolly assessed Ghemor. "I am ready."

"Ready?" he echoed. "Ready for what?

"When I was seven years old, you sent me to the Obsidian Order training facility. I asked if it was because I was a bad Cardassian."

"Yes?" Ghemor prompted impatiently.

"You said I was a good Cardassian, so good that you wanted me to explore my gifts in the proper setting. You said that someday I might be able to return the favor. For not sending me to a Terran slave camp."

Ghemor was increasingly intrigued by her uncanny calm. "Yes, I remember that."

"I have been in a slave camp," Seven told him. "I am ready to repay the favor."

"How?" Ghemor asked cautiously.

"With your backing, I can take over the position of Overseer."

Tain felt his heart leap within him. Agent Seven as the Overseer? It would be everything he had dreamed of, to have one of his agents at the helm of the Alliance. The only problem was . . . Seven was talking to Ghemor instead of him.

"That's impossible!" Ghemor exclaimed. "How could *you* be Overseer?"

"I have gained influential allies in the Alliance. They are ready to approve my appointment. Your support need only be tacit until the vote is called."

"What about Kira?"

"Kira will nominate me as her replacement."

Ghemor's eyes narrowed, and his pudgy fingers steepled beneath his chin. "Oh, she will? Didn't you just say she sold you to a slave camp?"

Seven assured him, "Kira will nominate me."

Ghemor didn't seem to believe her. "What does Enabran Tain say about this?"

Tain leaned closer, looking for any trace of a reaction in Seven. Guilt, maybe even resentment. But there was nothing.

"I am no longer an agent of the Obsidian Order," Seven said quietly.

Ghemor shook his massive head at that. "I'd like to see Tain's expression when he hears that."

"He is undoubtedly monitoring your channels," Seven told him. "So he already knows."

Tain's fingers tightened on the edge of his desk. She was good, too good. He didn't intend to let her go.

"No . . ." Ghemor protested, involuntarily checking his communications defense systems. "That's impossible. I have the best encryption node the Selerines can make. Tain couldn't break my security."

"Believe what you wish," Seven said flatly. "Will you back me as Overseer?"

Ghemor's eyes shifted as he considered it. He would be an idiot to refuse Seven's offer. If it came to nothing, he would lose nothing. Yet if she became Overseer, he stood to gain exponential power through an alliance with her.

"I'll do it," Ghemor agreed.

Seven showed no signs of relief or victory. "After Kira has resigned and named me as her replacement, the Regent will contact you for confirmation."

Seven signed off without another word. Tain could see Ghemor for a few seconds longer, until he closed the channel. Ghemor looked like a big man who had been run over by a hovercraft, dazed yet determined to get the person who did it. Apparently he was already considering how to take advantage of Seven when she became Overseer.

The signal came through on a secured agent's channel, breaking into Tain's rapid assessment of what had just happened. He had to check his implant chrono to discover he had been sitting for ninety microns without seeing the data flash by on his monitors.

Agent Seven appeared on the screen. *"So you know."*

"Yes," Tain said bluntly. "Why?"

"I will no longer kill at your command."

He should have brought her back when he saw the signs of deterioration. He could have stopped such a rapid decline with fresh programming. Perhaps it was not too late. . . .

"I have plenty of assassins," Tain dismissed. "You are much more valuable as Overseer."

"I will no longer be under your command," Seven patiently repeated.

"No, I can see you've risen higher than I could have hoped." Tain knew that only the truth would break through to her, and perhaps allow him get a fresh hold on her. "You are truly my equal." After a moment, he added, "There are few people I've told that."

Seven's lips tightened as if she wanted to say something, but refrained.

"You will be a fine Overseer," Tain continued, trying to soothe her. "A powerful ally for Cardassia. A powerful ally for the Obsidian Order."

"I have made an alliance with Ghemor," Seven reminded him.

"You know the truth, Seven. Once an agent, always an agent. You belong with us. You will die as part of the Obsidian Order."

"I'm no longer an agent. I have found my humanity. Now, I am Terran."

"You can do as you wish," Tain assured her. "You'll be a superb Overseer. But do not push me away. Meet with me so we can discuss your strategy and plans."

"No. I will speak to you only through subspace."

Tain sat back. Her blue eyes looked right into him; she was absolutely sure of herself. His assessment appeared to be right on at least one account.

"You have the portal." He didn't need to ask. The portal had always been the unknown factor in his calculations.

"*Yes.*" Seven lifted a round object that looked similar to a porthole on a ship. "*It is a portable Iconian gateway.*"

Tain felt a sudden tremor in his leg. He grabbed his thigh, preventing it from moving. One of the creeping signs of age that he usually refused to acknowledge.

An Iconian gateway . . .

"*I can look into it,*" Seven continued, "*and think of someone. The portal takes me there instantly, passing through time, space, and matter as if they don't exist. Light-years are nothing to the portal.*"

Suddenly, the walls of the bunker didn't feel so reassuring. Tain knew everything there was to know about Iconian technology. The shiny titalium of his bunker couldn't withstand the penetrative power of an Iconian gateway. His scientists had tried to duplicate the Iconian teleportation techniques for decades with no success.

If only he had known Kira's portal was Iconian . . . if only Seven had sent him an image of it. He would have ordered Agent Seven to steal it and return immediately. Was it too late?

"*You will let me go,*" Seven told him.

"I could reveal you as an Obsidian Order Agent," Tain reminded her.

For the first time, Seven faintly smiled. "*Then I would have to reveal the details of my prior missions. Including the assassination of Duras and Winn Adami, to name the most recent.*"

Tain had to admit she had him there. He forced himself to return her smile, a thin stretching of the lips. "Congratulations on your promotion, my dear."

Seven leaned closer for a moment, her cleft chin and the collar of her Cardassian pilot's jumper looming in the monitor before the signal ceased.

Tain swallowed, sitting very still in his chair. A slight ping behind him caused him to whirl, expecting to see the blue distortion of a phaser bolt shooting toward him. But Seven wasn't there.

He accessed everything Seven had reported about the portal before she knew it was Iconian. Apparently there was nothing to indicate imminent arrival through the portal, not a disturbance in the air or breath of sound. Seven said she had simply, instantly appeared.

His head turned, struck by shifting light. But it was only the data scrolling by on the screen.

Tain shivered, in the grip of something he couldn't control. His palms slipped on the metal armrest, so he clasped his hands together tightly in his lap, triggering his implant to perform an assessment of the situation.

When he raised his head, the old spymaster was once more in control of himself. But he knew he had been beaten by his own pupil. Seven was truly a product of his training, and she had proven herself a worthy adversary.

However, it was not over yet. Tain would triumph in the end. It had taken over ten standard years to eliminate Gul Dukat as a threat. Seven would be easier because he knew her inside and out. He had created her. As long as he didn't raise her suspicions and he cooperated, even praised her ingenuity, he could avoid a sudden deadly visit.

But someday, when Seven thought she was safe from him at last, he would show her that she still belonged to the Obsidian Order. She would know that she had lived and died as his agent.

Chapter 19

WORF'S MONTH OF self-imposed isolation ended when the last candle flickered out, sending up a twisting wisp of gray smoke. The room was dark and empty, never to hear Deanna's laughter or see her smile again.

Worf let out a roar of grief, more painful than the death howl that gloried in a fallen warrior. He was alone.

The exterior door slid aside. Traditional Betazoid mourning dictated that the loved ones were joined by friends of the deceased during the hour following the monthlong vigil.

It was B'Elanna, holding a *chitmus* leaf from Betazed. Worf staggered to his feet. "You come to honor Deanna."

B'Elanna sadly walked to the shrine and laid the leaf on the table among the smoldering candles. "How could I not?"

They stood together looking at Deanna's Cisterian

saber hanging on the wall, draped in the scarf that still carried her scent.

"Good-bye, my *Imzadi,*" Worf whispered. He kissed the edge of the blade, his huge hands splayed against the wall. Then he turned away. He couldn't stay in her room any longer.

B'Elanna followed him into his quarters, heading to the cabinet where he kept the finest bloodwine. She poured two flagons, as she had done dozens of other occasions. He sat in his favorite chair beneath the observation window, where he could watch the space spreading out before the *Negh'Var.* The orange arc of Mars was below, but he preferred to look at the stars, eager to return to space.

Somehow, it was finally over. His month of constant mourning had burned through him, leaving emptiness and a dull ache inside. He swallowed deep of the bloodwine.

They sat in silence for a considerable time. "You are the only one who came to honor Deanna," Worf finally said.

"Who else was as close to her as you and I?" B'Elanna asked. "You don't think Kira would come."

Worf furrowed his brow. "On Qo'noS I heard that Deanna had become . . . close to Kira Nerys."

"Rumors," B'Elanna repeated dismissively. "Deanna never trusted Kira."

"They spent time together," Worf said slowly. "Many nights together."

"Deanna would never betray you in her heart. She was convincing Kira to give her the gaming license for New Hope. Kira finally did." B'Elanna leaned forward. "But have you ever known Deanna to change her mind about someone? Her first impression was always infallible."

"True." Worf considered that. Deanna had instantly been attracted to him and had shown it from the first moment they met. . . . He had been a captain then, making routine sector checks for the Alliance when he discovered the beautiful Betazoid in an Orion spaceport. They had both known that they were meant for each other. Deanna's faith and love had never wavered.

Worf had relied on Deanna's judgment about people. She had trusted B'Elanna, and had convinced him that Duras's protégé was worth his time and interest. It wasn't long before he realized that B'Elanna was as pure as latinum, with courage and determination to match any Klingon's.

On the other hand, Deanna had never trusted K'mpec. She had warned him that the old man would betray him in the end. From the rumors on Qo'noS, Worf believed that K'mpec had dishonorably hired an assassin to kill Duras. Deanna had cleared Gowron of any involvement. That was the only reason Worf had agreed to make a pact of cooperation with the new High Chancellor.

B'Elanna reminded him, "Deanna was repulsed by Kira's excesses and her self-centered tantrums. She's incapable of loving anyone but herself. Deanna thought Kira was bad for the Alliance. She didn't vote for her as Overseer even though you asked her."

Worf grunted agreement. Deanna had shown reluctance whenever he mentioned Kira. She wasn't jealous, never that, but she sometimes seemed anxious about

Kira's presence on the *Negh'Var*. It was just like his *Imzadi* to befriend the Bajoran, thus gaining control over her.

"Deanna did not like Kira Nerys," he agreed.

"Kira has no honor," B'Elanna said, as if that explained everything. "She doesn't honor Deanna. She left two days ago to return to Bajor."

Worf growled low in his throat remembering the brazen way Kira had invaded his mourning. "No, Kira does not honor Deanna."

B'Elanna set down her bloodwine. "I wasn't going to mention this until later . . ."

"What?" Worf demanded.

"Most of the Intendants have agreed that Kira must be replaced. She is incompetent as Overseer. I found out that it hasn't been Kira managing the trade and production schedules. Seven did everything for her."

Worf had to think to place the name. "The Terran? Her pleasure slave?"

"Seven is a Free-Terran. Her foster father is Legate Ghemor, head of the Cardassian Detapa Council. He is backing her bid for Overseer."

Worf was astonished. "A Terran as Overseer?"

"I'm half-Terran," B'Elanna reminded him.

Worf took another swallow of bloodwine. "Your mother was Klingon."

"And Seven was raised by Cardassians." B'Elanna leaned forward. "But she was cast off, so she isn't loyal to them. I think she could be a useful ally as Overseer."

Worf couldn't imagine a Terran in the second-highest post in the Alliance. "A Terran . . ."

"If you appoint Seven as Overseer, then *you* ultimately stay in control."

"Precedent." Worf remembered how he had supported Kira in order to gain precedent. "The Regent appoints the Overseer."

"Seven has already proven herself. Kira tossed her out a month ago, and the shipping lines have become hopelessly tangled. Production is off by fifteen percent in every key market. You'll be lucky to get any latinum out of this quarter."

Worf sat forward. "Is this true?"

"I hate to bring you bad news, but it's affecting everyone. We have to do something."

Worf stood up, flinging aside his empty flagon. "Bring Seven to me."

Worf was pacing in his quarters, more than ready to return to his bridge. From here he could take his personal turbolift to any part of the *Negh'Var*. It felt as if a long time had passed, yet he slipped back into his ship with ease. He had never relinquished command.

B'Elanna entered with Seven, who strode forward to meet him. Her maroon pilot's jumper was Cardassian, subtly resembling an officer's uniform with its dramatic V from shoulders to waist. Perhaps to remind him that her foster father was head of the Detapa Council.

Yet Worf remembered the last time he had seen Seven. It was during one of Kira's "soirees" on Utopia

Planitia, the night before the *Negh'Var* had returned to the Klingon Empire for Gowron's confirmation. Seven had been wearing little more than hip boots and a chest plate, walking at the end of a golden chain held by Kira.

"*You* would be Overseer?" Worf sneered.

The Terran woman remained impassive. "I've been performing the Overseer's duties since Kira's tour began. During that period, until one month ago, production was up twenty-six percent. Since I left, production has fallen to eighty-four percent of the level prior to the appointment of the Overseer."

She sounded like a computer. Worf wished Deanna were here. What would she think of this Terran? B'Elanna certainly seemed to trust her.

"Go," he told B'Elanna. She instantly left his quarters.

Seven lifted her chin, waiting for him to speak first. That was good.

"I do not believe the Cardassians will vote for a Terran as Overseer," Worf said bluntly.

"Ghemor supports me because of our past relationship, and he has a majority on the Detapa Council. After Kira resigns, you can confirm his vote." She held out a disk. "This is his private channel."

Worf ignored her outstretched hand, pulling on the tops of his gloves, tightening them over his fingers as if preparing for a fight. "Kira Nerys will kill you for challenging her."

"Kira Nerys will nominate me as her successor," Seven countered.

Worf knocked her outstretched hand aside. "You lie!"

Seven was flung off balance, but as she turned, she shifted the disk to her other hand and whipped it around into Worf's face. They froze, the corner of the disk resting against his cheek. Worf had her wrist in an iron grip, but with a little more pressure, she could draw blood. Glaring at her, he had never seen such ferocity in blue eyes.

After a few moments, he began to chuckle, letting go of her wrist. She slowly pulled the disk away. They stepped back, looking at each other.

"So you are brave," Worf admitted. "But I will not agree to this."

Seven inclined her head. "It is your decision, Regent."

Worf was pleased with her obedience as she quietly waited for his dismissal. Maybe there was something to be said for dealing with a Terran. Kira had been arrogant and sometimes careless in her ways with him. This Terran appeared to be as sharp as a cracked whip.

Worf waved her away. "Go."

Seven went to the door and paused. "My condolences on your loss. I admired Deanna Troi, as did everyone I know."

Worf felt his anger rise at the mention of his *Imzadi,* but Seven's respectful acknowledgment tempered his reaction. He wanted people to speak of Deanna in this way. He did not want Deanna forgotten.

As the door closed behind her, Worf knew that he would agree to appoint Seven as Overseer. But only if Kira stepped down.

Chapter 20

In Kira's opinion, the first day after leaving the *Negh'-Var* was the worst. Despite the light-years rapidly accumulating between the *Siren's Song* and the Sol system, she knew she wasn't safe. Now that Seven had the Iconian portal, she could show it to Worf and accuse Kira of killing Deanna. Or Seven could pay her a sudden visit with a phase disruptor.

Now Kira wished she had put Seven in an airlock when she had the chance. How could she know the Terran would be so resourceful?

Kira posted four guards to surround her at all times, their phaser pistols held ready to fire on intruders. But it got tedious after a while. She didn't like them aiming their weapons at her, so they were trained on the ceiling. She entertained herself with drills to see how fast they could lower their weapons and fire. They stunned almost every one of her slaves before she finally tired of the game.

Besides, it would be smarter to send a slave through the Iconian portal carrying an explosive device. If Kira ever got the portal back, that's what she would do next time.

The constant waiting turned into nervous anticipation. It was truly stimulating not knowing when or where it would happen, but she was sure someone would make a move against her. She had arranged to pick up two fighter vessels and two long-range escorts in the Ennan system. Now she was glad B'Elanna hadn't given her the new ship she wanted. She wanted the crews to be loyal to her, as far as latinum could buy loyalty.

Kira was sitting on the waste-disposal unit when Seven arrived. Seven stunned Marani, and Kira watched helplessly as the slave slumped to the marble floor. Her own phaser pistol was lying on the basin, several feet away. The door was sealed.

Seven turned her phaser on Kira, tucking the Iconian portal under one arm. Her hair was pulled back tightly, bringing the lines of her face into stark relief.

Kira spread her hands wide. "You have me at a disadvantage."

Seven obviously didn't see the humor in the situation. She edged over and picked up Kira's tiny phaser pistol, slipping it into the thigh pocket of her maroon jumpsuit. Adjusting her hold on the portal, she gripped it with one hand, leaving it open as if prepared to leap through.

"Zip yourself up," she told Kira.

Kira slowly rose and rearranged her black skin-suit, smoothing it over her hips and chest. She kept glancing over at Seven. At one time, the Terran had been inflamed by the sight of her body. Now the mirrors repeated her image into infinity.

But Seven didn't react. "You will make an announcement to the Alliance relinquishing the Overseer's position."

"Or what?" Facing the mirrored wall, Kira adjusted her headband with the tips of her fingers. She could see Seven and the phaser repeated endlessly. "If you were going to kill me, I'd already be dead."

"Worf is the one you should be concerned about."

Kira raised one brow. Well, that was true enough. But at least it confirmed that Seven hadn't told Worf yet. If only she could get the phaser from her . . .

"How did you time it so well?" Kira asked, trying to distract her. "I've had guards around me every second."

"I pictured you sitting here, and I was brought to this time." Seven checked the chrono on the wall. "It's two hours earlier than when I left Sol."

"How clever of you to figure that out!" Kira drawled, finally turning around.

"I wondered why you never attempted time travel," Seven added. "With a device capable of transcending matter and space, one could reasonably assume that it was capable of transcending time."

Kira felt her patronizing smile slip. "Well, never mind all that. You're here, and that's what counts."

"You will make an announcement to the Alliance," Seven repeated.

"Yes, I know, abdicating as Overseer. Overworked, I suppose? I need to take a long vacation?" Kira nudged Marani on the floor, but the slave remained unconscious. Unfortunate.

Seven's beautiful face was serene. "You will publicly recommend me as your replacement."

Kira sucked her breath in. "What?!" she blurted out. "*You?* Overseer . . . that's absurd!"

"Both the Cardassians and the Klingons have agreed. The other Intendants will do anything to get rid of you." Seven briefly shook her head. "Your management skills are inadequate for the needs of the Alliance territories."

"Inadequate?" Kira repeated, completely amazed by her impertinence. "You're a *Terran!* A substandard species. How could you be Overseer?"

"I was acting as Overseer until you sold me as a mining slave."

Kira was truly taken aback. "I made the major decisions. You just handled a few details."

"Inaccurate." Seven leveled her phaser at Kira. "Apparently I must proceed to Plan B."

Kira drew back in spite of herself. "What's Plan B?" she had to ask.

"If you're dead, then a replacement will be needed." Seven's voice lowered. "I don't need your endorsement. Yet you have assisted me, however inadvertently. I would prefer to not kill you."

Kira knew Seven meant it. She was lucky Seven had given her this chance.

"So I abdicate, with you as my heir apparent?" Kira mussed. "I think I could live with that."

"You will make the announcement immediately," Seven told her.

"Surely I can have a few hours to settle my affairs," Kira said innocently.

"Immediately," Seven repeated. "Or I will return to you here, before you walk out that door, and this will end differently."

Seven held up the portal, her phaser aimed at Kira. Kira tried unsuccessfully to see who appeared in the mirror. "You haven't told B'Elanna?" Kira asked in alarm. B'Elanna would surely tell Worf.

"I have other allies," Seven said diffidently. "And now I will be Overseer."

Kira blinked. "Good girl. I didn't expect such sophistication from you—"

Seven disappeared through the portal.

It happened too fast. Everything seemed to fold in on itself. Seven was there one moment and gone the next. Kira didn't even have a chance to move. The abruptness was shocking.

Then she realized that if she didn't go out and immediately abdicate, Seven would reappear before she left the 'fresher to kill her. Her mind boggled at the time paradox, getting caught up in the temporal contradictions.

Kira scrambled at the cabinets in the 'fresher, but there was no weapon she could use to defend herself if

Seven returned. She knew she would have to be resolved to abdicate before she left the 'fresher, or Seven would reappear. She didn't mind splitting off alternate universes, but she didn't want to die in this one. Not when she had a chance to live and one day take back everything that Seven had stolen from her.

Yes, that was the right spirit. Kira stepped over the crumpled form of Marani, heading for the door. She would let it go for now, but one day, she would regain control of the former Terran Empire and would rule again. Kira was certain of that.

Chapter 21

THE ASTONISHMENT ON Kira's face as Seven abruptly teleported away was nothing compared to Janeway's expression when she returned. The redheaded Terran leaped back, clearly ready to defend herself if she needed to.

Seven shook her head, trying to clear it. Two teleports right after another had thoroughly disoriented her.

Janeway cautiously approached. She had watched Seven leave, and apparently only a few seconds later she had returned. "What was *that?*" Janeway demanded.

"I was finishing what needed to be done," Seven explained.

Seven went into her private chamber on her new starship, courtesy of B'Elanna and the Alliance. She quickly locked away the Iconian portal while Janeway was in the other room. She made it a point to learn from other people's mistakes. She wouldn't let anyone steal the portal from her as she had stolen it from Kira.

When she returned, Janeway was still standing. She was extremely tense, her arms tightly crossed as she nervously examined the room.

No wonder. Hardly an hour ago, B'Elanna had authorized Janeway's release from the mining complex, and Seven had beamed her directly aboard her new ship. Giving Janeway only enough time to change into a plain dark coverall, Seven had used her as the focal point for the teleportation.

Now Janeway was wary and suspicious. "What do you want from me?"

"I want the same thing that you want," Seven told her. "Freedom."

Janeway narrowed her eyes. "Prove it."

Inclining her head, Seven silently acknowledged that would be the most succinct course of action. "Follow me."

Seven noticed that Janeway remained tense as they walked through the empty corridors of her new ship *Voyager.* It was twice as large as Kira's cruiser, with long-range and high-speed capabilities. Seven had chosen this vessel because of its increased power capacity for defense and computation, rather than the one Kira had asked for, which had extensive cargo bays.

The transporter pads were behind a barrier where a forcefield could be activated. She operated the controls outside. With a few taps, she had clearance and passed her hand over the activation sequencer. Six Terrans materialized. They were wearing the rags provided by the mining complex, and they shielded their eyes from the too-bright lights. Chakotay cried out and pointed at Seven in recognition.

"My crew," Janeway softly exclaimed.

"Half of your crew," Seven corrected. "Please step off the pads."

Janeway urged the confused Terrans to move away. Another six Terrans appeared on the pads. Seven was pleased to note that that the last group included Beverly Crusher, the woman doctor she had met in the Pakled slave ship. She had specifically requested Crusher along with the rest of Janeway's crew.

As Seven locked down the transporter, the message she had been expecting arrived from B'Elanna. The bridge was only a step away, and the rest of the Terrans followed her. Quickly reviewing the message from the captain's chair, Seven knew she had won.

"What's going on here?" Janeway asked, standing next to her chair.

Seven put the message on the main screen so everyone could see it. B'Elanna's face suddenly loomed over them. Gasps rose from the Terrans who had been enslaved in the Sol system. Paris cried out, "No! We didn't do anything!"

But the recorded message from B'Elanna was already running. *"Seven, I thought you would like to see Kira's announcement that was just released, along with the Klingon and Cardassian endorsements."* The half-Klingon glanced down and smiled. *"I just got the first official complaint, from the Orion Intendant. Doubtless they'll say one of them should be Overseer instead of you. This won't be easy, but nothing is."*

B'Elanna's toothy grin faded and was replaced by the self-satisfied smirk of Kira Nerys. To Seven's experienced eye, she looked flushed. As if she had just been routed out of the 'fresher and ordered to leave the party.

"It is with great regret," Kira began with a dewy-eyed drawl. Seven rolled her eyes at the flowery language that followed. Kira was *"exhausted, simply exhausted"* but she believed she had *"established concrete systems of exchange"* that anyone could manage. In passing, she added *"My aide, Seven of Cardassia, has been most helpful . . . most helpful. I'm sure she could do a good job if given half a chance."*

Kira managed to sound as if she didn't really believe it. With a weary wave of her hand, indicating that the complete destruction of the Alliance was too much for her to bear right now, Kira added, *"I will be glad to return to my post at a later date."*

Seven knew that was a threat aimed directly at her. But she had expected as much. Her direct association with Cardassia would also set off alarms in many sectors, but she had expected that as well.

Kira's image faded back to the starfield. The gathered Terrans looked like they didn't know what was going on, except for Janeway. "You?" she asked incredulously. "You're going to be the new Overseer?"

"Yes." Seven watched their reactions, sadly noting that most of them seemed fearful.

Seven felt strangely adrift. Her implant database had provided her with the Klingon psychology she needed to interact successfully with Worf, offering data on when to parry his attack and when to yield. The database had also whispered the correct course of action when she dealt with her Cardassian foster father. She even knew exactly how to manipulate Enabran Tain, the man who had given her this knowledge over the years, filling her database with information on every known alien in the galaxy.

Except for Terrans.

Looking into Janeway's eyes, Seven knew she was on her own. "I brought you here because I have nothing. But with your help, I can become the Overseer of the former Terran Empire."

"*My* help?" Janeway asked incredulously. "That's impossible. How can a Terran be Overseer?"

"I will be Overseer." Seven said it with quiet conviction. "But I need a crew to staff this ship."

"You want my crew?" Janeway asked, obviously flattered.

"Will you be commander of this ship?" Seven asked. "And the others, will you be my helmsmen, my engineers?" She looked at Beverly Crusher. "My physician?"

Slowly they looked at one another, seemingly overwhelmed by the offer.

"As B'Elanna said, it will not be easy," Seven said. "Terrans are hated by the Alliance. One mistake, and we could be sent back to the mining complex. But now we have a chance to make a difference for ourselves and for other Terrans. Will you help me?"

Janeway was the first to step forward. "Yes," she declared. "I'll help you."

As the rest of the crew agreed, one after the other, their voices strong, Seven knew that she had won. With this ship and this crew, she would finally be free.

Look for STAR TREK fiction from Pocket Books

Star Trek®: The Original Series

Star Trek: The Next Generation®

Star Trek: Voyager®

Star Trek®: New Frontier

Star Trek®: Invasion!

Star Trek®: Day of Honor

#1 • *Ancient Blood* • Diane Carey
#2 • *Armageddon Sky* • L.A. Graf
#3 • *Her Klingon Soul* • Michael Jan Friedman
#4 • *Treaty's Law* • Dean Wesley Smith & Kristine Kathryn Rusch
The Television Episode • Michael Jan Friedman
Day of Honor Omnibus • various

Star Trek®: The Captain's Table

#1 • *War Dragons* • L.A. Graf
#2 • *Dujonian's Hoard* • Michael Jan Friedman
#3 • *The Mist* • Dean Wesley Smith & Kristine Kathryn Rusch
#4 • *Fire Ship* • Diane Carey
#5 • *Once Burned* • Peter David
#6 • *Where Sea Meets Sky* • Jerry Oltion
The Captain's Table Omnibus • various

Star Trek®: The Dominion War

#1 • *Behind Enemy Lines* • John Vornholt
#2 • *Call to Arms...* • Diane Carey
#3 • *Tunnel Through the Stars* • John Vornholt
#4 • *...Sacrifice of Angels* • Diane Carey

Star Trek®: The Badlands

#1 • Susan Wright
#2 • Susan Wright

Star Trek®: Dark Passions

#1 • Susan Wright
#2 • Susan Wright

Star Trek® Books available in Trade Paperback

Omnibus Editions
    Invasion! Omnibus • various
    Day of Honor Omnibus • various
    The Captain's Table Omnibus • various
    Star Trek: Odyssey • William Shatner with Judith and Garfield Reeves-Stevens

Other Books

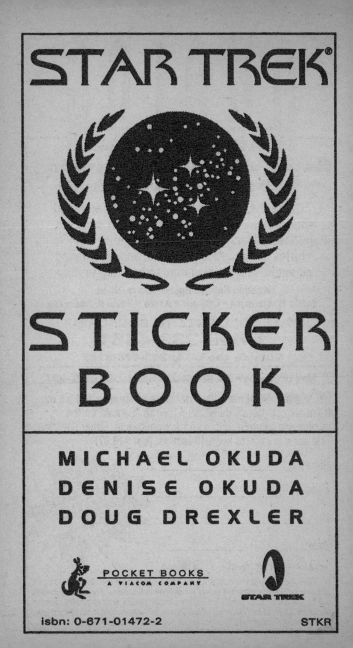

STAR TREK®

STICKER BOOK

MICHAEL OKUDA
DENISE OKUDA
DOUG DREXLER

POCKET BOOKS
A VIACOM COMPANY

STAR TREK

isbn: 0-671-01472-2   STKR

Sɪx centuries,
ten captains.
One proud tradition.

STAR TREK®
ENTERPRISE LOGS

INCLUDES STORIES FROM

Diane Carey
Greg Cox
A.C. Crispin
Peter David
Diane Duane
Michael Jan Friedman
Robert Greenberger
Jerry Oltion
and
John Vornholt

STAR TREK

AVAILABLE NOW FROM POCKET BOOKS

ENTL

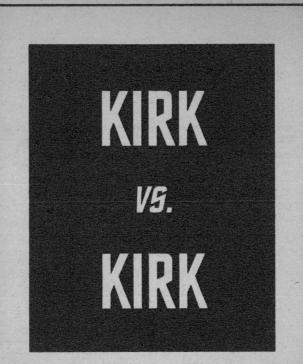

KIRK

vs.

KIRK

STAR TREK®
PRESERVER

A novel by William Shatner
Available now from Pocket Books